THE
FAR SIDE OF
HAPPINESS

Gerry Boland

THE
FAR SIDE OF
HAPPINESS

ARLEN
HOUSE

The Far Side of Happiness

is published in 2018 by
ARLEN HOUSE
42 Grange Abbey Road
Baldoyle, Dublin 13, Ireland
Phone: 00 353 85 7695597
arlenhouse@gmail.com
arlenhouse.blogspot.com

Distributed internationally by
SYRACUSE UNIVERSITY PRESS
621 Skytop Road, Suite 110
Syracuse, NY 13244–5290
Phone: 315–443–5534; Fax: 315–443–5545
supress@syr.edu
syracuseuniversitypress.syr.edu

ISBN 978–1–85132–174–2, paperback

cover image 'Vocal Sadness' by Susan Mannion
is reproduced courtesy of the artist
www.yewtreestudio.ie

CONTENTS

6   *Acknowledgements*

9   First Cigarette

15   Bridie's Birthday Party

27   A Short Drive to the Shops

36   Only a Conversation Away

42   The Caller

49   The Man with No Name

55   Carlow

63   Who Knows Bernard Ashe?

72   A Moment of Clarity

80   Watching *The Virginian*

88   Bully

94   Making Sandwiches

103 Begin with Loneliness

112 A Woman Like That

123 A Surprise Party

131 The Far Side of Happiness

138 *About the Author*

'A Short Drive to the Shops' was published in *Southword*, Issue 32 (July 2017).

An earlier version of 'The Man with No Name' was placed third in the Francis MacManus Short Story Competition in 2008 and was broadcast on RTÉ1.

'A First Cigarette' was placed third in the 2011 Writing4All Competition, judged by Christine Dwyer-Hickey.

'The Caller' was published in the *Cúirt Annual*, 2007.

'Bridie's Birthday Party' was runner-up in the 2009 Fish International Short Story Award, judged by Colum McCann, and was included in the *Fish Anthology* in that same year.

Thanks to Roscommon County Council (Arts Office and Library) for providing financial assistance which has made the publication of this book possible, and thanks also to Roscommon County Council Arts Office for providing a number of bursaries for periods at the Tyrone Guthrie Centre in Annaghmakerrig, where many of these stories were written.

A special thanks to Joe Boland and to Paddy Keogh who read the stories and who gave insightful and invaluable feedback. The collection is stronger and more complete as a result of their input and generosity.

THE
FAR SIDE OF
HAPPINESS

First Cigarette

What shocks him is how quickly his life has unravelled. He had thought of himself as being well integrated, with plenty of friends and a job he enjoyed, with work colleagues he liked. Now he has no one.

He throws the bedclothes aside and slides his feet into his slippers and walks to the windowsill and turns off the alarm. There is a thin layer of frost on the outside of the windowpanes. He takes his dressing gown down from the hook on the back of the door and puts it on, pulling it tight and tying a loop-knot with the cord.

And now he does something unexpected. Instead of going into the kitchen, to the relative warmth of the overnight storage heater, he unlocks the front door and steps out into the frosty morning. Immediately, there is a sudden shriek and an urgent flapping of large wings. The pheasant swoops low and with an awkward elegance down to the bottom of the meadow and lands and disappears behind some fruit bushes. Now he is fully awake. He isn't sure who got the biggest scare, he or the pheasant.

There is a pair of them. He's been feeding them throughout the arctic winter just passed, and the pheasants have become daily celebrants at the small feast he leaves out around the side of the house. Sometimes he looks out his living-room window and the two of them are standing on the low wall that divides the small front garden from the meadow, completely still, taking in everything, every sound, every movement, seemingly at peace and relaxed, but never that, never what they seem, for they cannot let their guard down, not for an instant; there are too many predators at large to take any chances.

It is a cold morning, but the sky is clear, and there is a hint of rare promise in the thin February air. He can go back indoors and get depressed, or he can step out into the fresh morning, suppressing his negative thoughts for a while. And so he walks down his driveway in his slippers and his dressing gown and the air is sharp and stinging in the still morning.

A feint suggestion of a long abandoned sense of renewal comes to him, from where he does not know. Perhaps it is the fact of being out so early that brings it on, but he finds himself thinking about the possibility of doing something completely different, a reinvention of himself, a new beginning. There are people out there who are in a far worse situation than he is. He owns his house. He has no mortgage to pay, no rent. That is a gift he should be thankful for. He knows of several couples who would do anything to be free of their mortgage; better still, to be entirely free, with no children, no school fees, no new clothes and school uniforms to buy, no food for a hungry family to be put on the table every day, when there is no money coming in.

Maybe I can start afresh.

He allows the thought rest there for a while, letting it sit, letting it settle.

At the bottom of the drive he stops and draws the cold air into his nostrils. It is foolish to be doing this, to be out on such a chilly morning in his dressing gown, and not a hat on his head or a scarf around his neck. He is normally careful about these things. He is prone to colds, to full-blown flu, and he is a bad patient, going out of his way to feel sorry for himself. But there is something unfamiliar and liberating about being down here at the end of his driveway, in his slippers and pyjamas and dressing gown. Watching out for the pheasant, who by now will probably be in the next field. The fruit bushes he planted the year before last have done better than expected in the peaty soil and have survived the coldest winter on record. Soon, tiny green leaves will begin to appear and in no time there will be flowers, and after that will come the blackcurrants and redcurrants, the raspberries and gooseberries and jostaberries. In a few years the bushes will be producing far too much fruit for him to use, unless he makes jam, which he isn't fond of, which of course is typical of him, to plant over twenty fruit bushes when all he really needs is five or six. He is always doing stupid things like that. He has never been much good at thinking things through to their inevitable conclusion.

A car horn beeps, and he waves at the driver, who he doesn't recognise. After the previous quiet, here are two more cars sweeping down the narrow road towards him. He recognises both cars, and immediately regrets having come down here in his dressing gown. Both drivers raise a hand as they pass, and both are unable to contain their curiosity, turning their heads a second time as they are passing, to get a better look. He catches a rare smile on the face of Joe Dunne as he goes by. He'll be on the phone to Margaret, his nosey, unpleasant windbag of a wife, before he reaches the end of the road.

'Luke McCormack has lost the plot, Mags. Take a trip down the road quick. He's away with the fairies down at the bottom of his drive, dressed for bed. Quick now, before he goes'.

She'll be all ears from her perch at her kitchen window. He wouldn't be a bit surprised if she hopped in her car and drove full belt down the road to have a look, on the pretence of going to the shops. With that thought in his head, he turns and walks back up the driveway.

He stops to examine the willows he stuck in the ground last year. Four of them have taken, but the rest are dead in the water, literally, for he knows from a conversation he had a few days ago with a local basket maker that he stuck them too deep in the boggy ground. He climbs the rest of the drive and is reaching with his outstretched palm to push open the front door when he hears a screech of brakes, followed by a thud, and a sudden, abrupt scream. Instinctively, he turns and runs down the drive, losing both slippers near the bottom. The braking and the thud and the scream came from not far away, perhaps up at the first bend, that's what he thinks, but when he reaches the road he sees that it is much closer.

The pheasant is lying on the road a hundred metres away. Margaret stands over it, a hand to her mouth. Only now, as he begins to walk towards the car, Margaret, the pheasant, does he realise he is in his bare feet. All he can think of is the other pheasant, and where she is. It is the male that is lying on the road, the one he startled less than fifteen minutes ago and who disappeared from sight at the bottom of the meadow. As he gets nearer, he notices that it isn't dead, for its head is moving slightly from side to side, as if the bird knows he is approaching and that he better get the hell out of there or the game is up. But the game is up, anyway. There is no chance it can walk away, let alone fly away after receiving such an almighty whack from the bumper of Margaret's car, which had probably been travelling at speed so she wouldn't miss the spectacle at the bottom of the drive. Well, here is the spectacle walking towards her, and he can see she is caught between the shock of what she has done and the strangeness of her near neighbour walking along the road in bare feet and in a white dressing gown.

He feels sick to the stomach that the morning has turned out like this. He was on the brink of some kind of breakthrough just a few minutes ago, intangible as it was. Something about a new start. Something about a pair of pheasants he'd fed over the winter and who were survivors.

And now this stupid woman has killed one of the pheasants, and the one left behind will have to cope on her own, and whatever chance there ever was of being trusted by those two mysterious birds, that is all gone up in smoke. It lies breathing its last on the road as he watches Margaret reach for a packet of cigarettes in the pocket of her bright blue dressing gown, take two out, light them both and hand one to him, even though he doesn't smoke, has never smoked. But he takes the cigarette all the same and he pulls on it as he knows smokers do, and he draws the deathly fumes deep into his lungs, as he also knows smokers do.

'I wasn't sure if you smoked or not', she says, to which he replies, 'I don't', and he turns his back on her and on the now dead pheasant and walks in his bare feet and dressing gown back along the road. He is heading for the shed at the back of the house, where he keeps his shovel. He will carry it back to where the pheasant is lying on the cold tarmacadam and he will give it a decent burial.

He is halfway up his drive when he remembers that the shovel was stolen last week, one day when he was out, and someone must have called, and seeing the place deserted, helped himself to his garden tools, his water hose, three bags of coal. 'The times that are in it', the postman had offered the next morning. 'Nothing's safe anymore'.

Back in the house, he dresses, then walks to where the pheasant lies, but it is no longer on the road. Margaret has departed the scene of the tragedy, but not before dumping the pheasant into the ditch, where it lies half-submerged in the muddy water, sodden and inert, a pitiful bundle of flesh and feathers. It is as good a place as any for it to be, he decides. Better, in fact, than a stupid burial. There are hungry mammals that will find it when darkness overcomes the daylight. It will keep whoever finds it ahead of the posse for a few more days.

As he walks back towards the entrance to his drive, his eye is turned by a movement in the field on his left. The female prowls the flattened grass, twenty metres from where he has stopped. She appears to be oblivious to his presence, a state utterly alien to her being. She is moving slowly towards the place where her companion lies. A part of him would like to follow her, to observe her reaction when she gets there, perhaps even as a way of acknowledging her inexplicable loss. But a larger part of him is repulsed by what has happened, and by what is now taking place, the search for and the finding of her dead companion. It is too terrible to think about, so he doesn't, and instead quickens his pace and within minutes is undressed and back in his by now cold bed.

Something has slipped away, has left him stranded, more alone than ever. He thinks that if he can get back to sleep he might be able to rid himself of the feeling that he knows has the potential to send him on a downward spiral that he is badly prepared for, even though he has felt it coming for days. But for that to happen, he needs to sleep. He lies beneath the covers and he knows that these are the times when sleep is elusive.

Bridie's Birthday Party

Francis Torpey lived in a small flat on the top floor of an old apartment block in the centre of the city. He had a job that forced him out into an intimidating and unpredictable world five days a week, but otherwise he kept to himself, never going out and, being solitary by nature and necessity, never having guests around.

Once a week his sister Patricia would pay him a visit, usually on a Friday evening, on her way home after five o'clock mass in Clarendon Street Church. She always rang to let him know she was on her way, for there was no intercom in the building and the door downstairs was always locked. At the appointed time, Francis would raise the lower part of the window and drop the key, neatly tied up in a clean sock, down to her.

This throwing down of the key was new. For fifteen years, whenever Patricia called, he skipped down the block's sixty-eight concrete stairs, taking two and often three steps at a time, to let her in. He descended soundlessly and with remarkable lightness of foot to avoid alerting his busybody neighbours who, he was convinced, spent their days listening out for his footsteps. A year ago, he failed to tend to a bad cold and, with dismaying rapidity, it entered his chest and floored him. He didn't get out of bed for a fortnight, except to answer Patricia's phone calls and, if her call was to tell him that she'd be downstairs in five minutes, to throw the keys down. When he was well again, he realised he no longer needed to go down – and back up – all those stairs. The keys would go out the window from now on.

This small change left a mark on Francis, who felt liberated by the experience. It was as if a long and strongly-held taboo had simply withered through a forced change in behaviour. He began to wonder what other aspects of his rigidly-contained life he might be able to alter.

He was a creature of many habits and obsessions. When he let himself in to his flat in the evenings, he would take care to double-lock the mortice lock he'd had installed the day he moved in. He would remove the keys from the lock and place them in a little wicker basket that he kept on the mantelpiece. More often than not, having placed the keys in the basket, some compulsion would bring him back within a matter of minutes. He would take the keys out, go to the door, put the key in the lock, and double-check that it was secure. Hardly a night went by that he didn't return to the door half-a-dozen times.

This he now stopped doing. If the door is locked the first time, he told himself, it will be locked every time I check it. How many times, he asked, have I discovered that I had forgotten to lock the door when I came in? He smiled, and caught himself in the act of smiling in the mirror above the mantelpiece, when he mouthed the answer to his question: *None.* He looked at his face in the mirror. *None,* he mimed. His thin pale face broke into a grin. 'None!' he mimed, except this time he forgot to mime, and the word shot out of his mouth in a shout. He began to laugh and found that he couldn't stop. He couldn't remember when he had ever laughed before.

The next morning, as he descended the stairs on his way to work in O'Shaughnessy's of Aungier Street, where he had worked as a mender of trousers and jackets for twenty-two years, he came across Mr Pelly ascending the stairs after a ten-hour shift up at the brewery. Mr Pelly lived with his wife, Nora, on the third floor. When he and Nora moved into the block six years ago, they had gone out of their way to be friendly to Francis, who they saw as a harmless little man afflicted by a crippling shyness. But over time, Francis' awkwardness wore them down, so that now when either of them passed him on the stairs, they simply said hello and moved quickly by, for Francis' shyness had made them equally shy of him.

John Pelly was tired and in poor form. Less than an hour ago he learned that he had been passed over for promotion. The news had come as a blow. Promotion would have meant no more shift work and a good deal more money. John thought that he might as well give in his notice and go back to work on the ships. At least then he'd be away from the accusing eyes of Nora, who was bound to take the news badly. That is why he didn't give a damn about Francis Torpey's insufferable shyness this particular morning, and when Francis stopped in the middle of the flight of stairs and extended his right hand towards him, something he had never done before in his life, John Pelly brushed angrily past, muttering an oath under his breath. The wide grin, which had lit up Francis' face in the shadowy stairwell, quickly faded.

'John Pelly, go back down those stairs and shake Mr Torpey's hand'.

It was the fearsome Nora Pelly who, upon hearing the main door down below bang shut and assuming it to be her husband home from work with good news, had opened her door in time to see the extraordinary incident on the stairwell. The sharpness of his wife's tone acted like a slap in the face and snapped John Pelly out of his self-absorption.

'Mr Torpey, please come back up the stairs and shake my husband's hand', Nora Pelly called down.

By now, doors had opened below and above, drawn to the commotion on the stairwell. Bridie and Majella leaned their fat forearms on the iron banisters of the fourth floor and looked down with incredulity at what they were witnessing: Francis Torpey, the man of no words and no personality, the man who would run a mile rather than engage in conversation, the man who *couldn't* converse, was beaming broadly and enthusiastically shaking John Pelly's hand. More astonishingly, he was speaking.

'A very good morning to you Mr Pelly, and to you Mrs Pelly'.

Looking up, he called, 'Good morning to the Cassidy sisters. I hope you all have a pleasant day. I'll knock on your door when I come home'.

He skipped down the remaining stairs as if he were a young man on his way to a football final.

Over the following months, Bridie and Majella, who lived directly below Francis, began to notice a change in their neighbour who, from the day he moved in, had maintained a fiercely-guarded privacy, never stopping to chat to any of the tenants whom he happened to come across on the landings. A whispered 'good day' or 'good night' was as much as most of the tenants ever got out of him. When he did find himself cornered, usually by widow O'Reilly, who lived in the large flat on the ground floor, he would edge backwards into the corner of the hallway and mutter a few sentences that widow O'Reilly, who had poor hearing at the best of times, was unable to make out.

'Can you not speak clearer, Mr Torpey?' she would say to him, driving him further back into the shadows of the dark, grey hallway. Later, she would stand at her open door and wait, all day if that is what it took, to detain each of the tenants and recount in full the one-way conversation she had had with 'the odd man up above us'.

He no longer spent every evening at home in his small flat, dining instead in local restaurants and pubs. He chanced a glass or two of wine, when he saw someone at an adjoining table drinking. He took up smoking, though he gave it up a week later, dismissing it as a filthy habit.

His conversations on the landings of the block, which were becoming a daily occurrence, seemed to the tenants forced and artificial. They couldn't comprehend the change that had come over him. He became the main topic of conversation. The tenants were pleased for him that he had overcome his appalling shyness, but they were also concerned for his sanity. Someone suggested, though not to him, that he should see a doctor. For the first time in living memory, there was a sense of communal concern, of a shared experience and a common purpose. Yet no one thought to pay a visit to the fifth floor tenant. Indeed, the very notion of getting any closer than was necessary to Francis Torpey was unthinkable.

As the months passed, the tenants, becoming bored by the banal pleasantries forced upon them by Francis, began to withdraw. Widow O'Reilly on the ground floor took to avoiding him, making sure her door was closed during the times Francis left for work and when he came home. Often, he would ring the doorbell anyway, but increasingly she would have the TV turned down and she would stand behind the door, waiting for him to go. John Pelly would have been open to humouring him, however Nora, who was by now sick to the teeth of Mr Torpey knocking on her door and talking non-stop until she'd have to tell him something was burning, or that she was late for church, couldn't tolerate his daily intrusions anymore and told her husband to steer clear of 'that insufferable little man' and not to be encouraging him. Only the Cassidy sisters continued to be friendly towards him and, being the two of them, they could always take turns in humouring him. In any case, Bridie noted, 'he seems to be going back in on himself, so he does'.

Up in his small flat, Francis was indeed going back into himself, but where he was going was not where he had come from. Now he might spend the entire evening in front of the mirror, playing out the next day's conversations in his head, replaying those of earlier in the day. He acted out the parts of each of the Cassidy sisters, of John and Nora Pelly, of old widow O'Reilly. He discovered something about himself that he never knew. How could he have known, considering he had never been a talker? Yet here he was, pretending to be widow O'Reilly, and the voice that came out of his mouth was the voice of the widow herself. He even had her peacock posture and her affected mannerisms.

'Can you not speak clearer, Mr Torpey? I'm blue in the face and me ears are burning trying to hear whatever it is you're saying. Did your mother or your father never teach you to talk proper?'

Such a cruel woman, Francis thought. And so ignorant, taking me for an *amadán* just because I was too shy to talk. He was fond of the two Cassidy sisters, and when he pretended to be them, he didn't have bitter or resentful thoughts.

'Lovely morning, Mr Torpey'.

'Lovely morning altogether, Mr Torpey'.

As he played the two parts, he moved from one side of the mirror to the other, adopting slight variations in body language to accommodate the dialogue and to match whichever sister he was playing.

'Yer lookin well. This time of the year suits you, doesn't it, Mr Torpey?'

'Didn't Mr Torpey tell us he likes this time of year, Bridie?'

He developed a wide range of characters. He had all the tenants, the rent man, the postman, the cleaner, the news seller on the corner, all the staff over at O'Shaughnessy's and most of the regular customers. He enjoyed it all so much it replaced his previous obsessions. He no longer bothered to check that the door was locked, often forgetting to lock it at all. The impeccable neatness of his wardrobe and his chest of drawers changed over the course of several weeks to a casual untidiness that resulted in his clothes being strewn everywhere, even in the small kitchen. He no longer washed any dishes or cutlery or pots or pans and soon took to grabbing a ready-made meal on the way home.

One morning, Bridie stopped him on the stairs.

'I always have a few friends around for my birthday, Mr Torpey. This year, on account of me turning seventy an' all, and you coming out of your shell like you have, well we'd both like it if you would come along. Around eight. No need to bring anything, except a few bottles of stout, if that's what you drink'.

'It's wine I drink now, Miss Cassidy'.

'O, how very posh, Mr Torpey. Bring along a nice bottle of wine for yerself, so. There'll be sandwiches and cake to beat the band. We'll have a good night. We always do. Do you sing, Mr Torpey?'

'No, Miss Cassidy, I've never sung in my life. I'll be happy to listen, though. I used to love listening to the old songs, I did'.

He left for work feeling elated, but by the time he arrived back at his flat, he had lost his earlier enthusiasm. Conversing with people he knew on the landings was one thing: being in a room full of people, some of whom he probably wouldn't know, seemed a step too far. He stood in front of the mirror and he held a mock conversation between himself and Majella Cassidy.

'Please explain to your sister, Miss Cassidy, that I am not at all well, that I won't be able to attend her birthday party'.

'Ah don't be silly, Mr Torpey, of course you'll come. Bridie would be terribly upset, she would'.

'I'm too sick, Miss Cassidy'.

'You're not sick at all, Mr Torpey. You're just a wee bit shy of all us women. Don't you worry yourself about it, we're not the biting kind'.

'O Miss Cassidy, you're a terrible woman. But honestly, I can't come. I'd only infect you all'.

'What is it you have, Mr Torpey?'

'I think it's a dose of malaria, Miss Cassidy. Either that or the plague'.

'Jesus Mary and Holy Saint Joseph, will you go back to your room right away Mr Torpey and don't come out till you're sure you're better. We wouldn't any of us be wanting to catch a dose of one of them diseases'.

'I will, Miss Cassidy, I will'.

Francis giggled just like Majella Cassidy giggled sometimes. The little play made him feel much better. He decided to open the bottle of wine that he had bought on his way home. Before he knew it, he had two glasses drunk. He was about to pour again when the doorbell rang.

'Mr Torpey! Mr Torpey! We're waiting for you downstairs'. It was Majella Cassidy.

'I'll be down in a minute, Miss Cassidy', he called out.

'Give us an old song, Mr Torpey!' squawked Bridie Cassidy, already half tipsy from the three gin-and-tonics she'd swallowed. 'Majella told us you have a lovely singing voice, isn't that right, Majella?'

'I said no such thing, Mr Torpey', Majella Cassidy said. She had gone a pure crimson from the mortification of it all. She could have killed her sister for saying such a thing. Every year it was the same, Bridie losing the run of herself and making a fool of everyone, most of all herself.

'Ara, go on Mr Torpey, sing a song for Bridie on her birthday', said Mrs Flanagan, who lived in a flat in the adjoining block and who knew the Cassidy sisters from childhood.

Francis was feeling a little tipsy. When he'd entered the room earlier, the crowded room silenced whatever pleasantries he was planning to make. All those faces staring up at him made him swallow his tongue. But Majella Cassidy had been very kind and attentive and had seen at once the discomfort he was in.

'This here is Mr Torpey from upstairs', she announced to the gathering. 'He's a lovely man and a good neighbour. We're lucky to have you above us, Mr Torpey'.

Someone said 'here here!' and someone else called out, 'you're very welcome, Mr Torpey', and this calmed him down and when Majella Cassidy showed him to a nice armchair over near the window and he sat down and looked around him, he could see that the room wasn't crowded at all. There was Bridie, over by the fireplace, and Nora and John Pelly on the sofa, and Mrs Flanagan beside them. They all smiled at him and he smiled back. Someone took the bottle of wine from his clammy hands and came back a minute later with a full glass and handed it to him. A ring on the doorbell brought three more people: the Carrolls from the second floor, and widow O'Reilly, who looked worn out from all the stairs.

'Someone give me a drink before I collapse', she said with her usual drama, and everyone laughed.

The atmosphere in the room tilted this way and that over the course of the next couple of hours, with the drink tilting it one way and the non-drinkers tilting it back again.

After two hours had passed, the drinkers took control of the evening and the non-drinkers were noisily pushed to the side. Mr Torpey was a quiet man who had latterly become garrulous, only to become quiet again. Everyone in the room knew that about him. His quiet demeanour at the party seemed to confirm his quiet status, which is why Bridie's thoughtless persistence that he should sing a song was greeted with much interest. All were curious to see if Mr Torpey would fold under the pressure, and if he did, what song would the quiet little man sing? Finally, following repeated verbal prodding by Bridie, Francis rose from his armchair by the window and made his way to the centre of the floor.

'Mr Torpey's taking centre stage', John Pelly boomed in the manner of a music hall compere.

'Is it opera you're going to sing, Mr Torpey?' Bridie called out, laughing. 'Majella says Mr Torpey has a voice that would have put John McCormack out of business'.

'Bridie, for heaven's sake, will you ever leave Mr Torpey alone?' said Majella, though she, too, couldn't help herself laughing at the sight of their odd neighbour standing in the middle of her living room, looking for all the world as if the floor was about to swallow him up.

'Belt it out Count McCormack!' cried Nora Pelly, who was full with drink.

Francis cleared his throat, pirouetted on one heel and, looking at Majella Cassidy, put on his Bridie voice.

'It's opera Mr Torpey is going to sing. Majella says he has a voice that would have put John McCormack out of business'.

The room became suddenly quiet, except for Majella, who started to giggle. She stopped abruptly when Mr Torpey pirouetted on his heel and laid his eyes on her sister.

'Bridie, will you ever leave Mr Torpey alone? Bridie, will you stop embarrassing us all? Bridie, do you not think you've drunk enough gin for one night? It's making you sound as common as muck'.

You could hear a pin drop in the room now. Francis had the accents and the characterisations uncannily perfect. They were not of a complimentary nature, yet to Francis they were as he saw them and as he heard them. There was no malice in his mimicry, but he was so accurate in catching the character and the voice that everyone in the room was shocked and embarrassed. No one likes to see themselves in all their rough normality paraded before their friends. Especially by someone who until this evening was a hopeless case.

He did them all. John Pelly. Nora Pelly. Widow O'Reilly. Mrs Flanagan. He couldn't be stopped. He drew a few nervous laughs when he did the postman and the rent man, but these imitations were short. Most of the hours in front of his mirror upstairs had been spent imitating the people he saw every day. The wine had given his performance a confidence and a freedom that brought a sharp edge to the material. For everyone present, it was too close to the bone. It was Majella who managed to close the curtains on the little show, by her tears. The strangeness of Mr Torpey's behaviour frightened her. She no longer felt safe in the same room as him. Everyone thought that she had been upset by his cruel mimicry, but when Nora Pelly put her arms around her, saying, 'Don't mind Mr Torpey, he's only teasing', she brushed her aside and bawled, 'I don't want him here. Get him out of here!' She became hysterical, and her screaming brought Francis' performance to an abrupt end.

'Best if you went back home, Mr Torpey', John Pelly said. 'You've upset too many people here tonight'.

'Mr Torpey'.

'Yes, Majella'.

'Mr Torpey, you are never to leave this flat again'.

'I won't, Majella. I won't even open the door'.

The curtains hung open and the glow of the city illuminated the dark room just enough for Francis to be able to see his reflection in the mirror. He moved from left to right, from right to left, in rhythm with the conversation. An ambulance siren echoed impatiently, angrily through the streets five floors below. Rain fell. It was well past midnight.

'Mr Torpey'.

'Yes, Majella'.

'Mr Torpey, you are never to leave this flat again'.

'I won't, Majella. I won't even open the door'.

The door of the Cassidy sisters flat opened, and muffled voices bid a solemn goodnight. Bridie had sobered up, and Majella sobbed quietly before the door closed again and there was silence from below.

'Mr Torpey'.

'Yes, Majella'.

'Mr Torpey, you are never to leave this flat again'.

'I won't, Majella. I won't even open the door'.

He was still in front of the mirror when dawn broke, moving one way, then the other.

A Short Drive to the Shops

Veronica

We called him Adam because he was our first, and because Rory liked the name. I wasn't keen on it, but I was happy to go along with whatever he chose. After all, it was Rory who'd made all the running in our on-again off-again relationship, who'd pursued the idea of marriage until he'd worn me down. And it was Rory, the desperate-to-be-father, who persuaded me to have a child. The motherly urge had never been a strong internal force, unlike my little sister who was a mother before she was twenty-one and who had four kids in five years. Not for me that kind of carry on; I was happy as I was, a working wife with a life.

The birth was the easy part. It was afterwards, when I brought him home, that the trouble started, the trouble being that my instincts had been right, I was not a natural mother. I became depressed for the first time in my life. Retreated to my bedroom and left him crying in his cot until he gave up on me. Went through confusing phases of loving him and resenting him, spoiling him and ignoring him, all in the space of a single day. And yet – and this is the most amazing thing – he turned out to be a good boy, so serene and seemingly contented. And because he was so calm I got used to the whole mother thing as we went along. He was always a little wary underneath this calmness he presented to us, which was understandable. I knew that I was the primary source of that.

The bike he was on that day had been a birthday present from both of us. He'd had us worn out with his pleadings for a bike. Our son was only eight, Rory said. Eight is too young to be cycling on the roads. He wouldn't be cycling on the roads, I argued. There would be a strictly-enforced rule that he would only go out on the roads if Rory was with him.

Let's be honest. I didn't really believe that Adam would keep to the footpaths. He had, even at that young age, started to play by his own rules. He was a clever boy, he saw how his father and his mother were using him for their own petty, vindictive purposes, each one pretending to be the more reliable, the more attentive, the more loving parent. I think even by the age of five he had begun to see through the charade, and by eight he had decided to make up his own rules.

So, even as I was pressing home my arguments to buy him a bike, part of me was aware that I was doing nothing more than getting back at Rory. For what? I can no longer remember. Something trivial, no doubt. Christ knows what kind of bitch I was then, a slave to conflict, up for a fight at any time of the day or night, hurling insults at Rory, who was no slouch himself when it came to confrontation.

And Adam, always in the middle, or up in his bedroom, working out his own survival strategies.

When our son asked for a bike, and his father emitted an emphatic 'No', he would not have been surprised to hear his mother say 'Yes'. Oh, he knew how to work us alright, our darling, manipulative son.

I blame myself and no one else for Adam's death. I do feel sorry for Molly Dunne. I genuinely do. Poor woman, she was devastated. Who wouldn't be? You're driving your car to the shops, along a road you travel everyday. The weather is fine. You have no worries, and a boy on a bicycle appears from nowhere in front of your car and before you can brake, you hear a sickening thud as a small human being made of flesh and blood and bones and soft tissue smacks against your windscreen and bounces over the roof and he's gone. Molly Dunne said at the inquest that she wasn't sure what had happened had really happened, it was that sudden, that impossible. She said you don't expect a boy on a bike to come out of nowhere, you don't expect to kill a young boy on your way to the shops. She told the coroner that she believed she was a safe driver. She said she always paid attention. She was in tears most of the time. Rory smelled a rat, he said there was something about Molly Dunne that he didn't like. I believe it was grief, a hideous, unbearable grief that made him suspect her of something, even though he couldn't articulate what it was, didn't *know* what it was. There was nothing rational about his hatred of her. It was pure and raw and unnervingly real. He wanted to go up to where she was sitting and put his hands around her neck and squeeze the life out of her. His reaction was almost as grotesque as the accident itself.

He's over it now. Well, maybe not over it, he'll never be able to forgive Molly Dunne, that's for certain, and he will always hold a special place in his heart for Adam. I do know that he's not so callow as to wipe the memory of his son in order to survive, but it would be true to say that he is in a far more positive place than I am or am likely to be for the foreseeable future. Me getting pregnant again has helped him to direct his gaze forward, towards an ideal that he believes we had conspired to destroy but which now seems possible: that is, the two of us united, something that seemed unlikely in the immediate aftermath of Adam's death.

We'd tried hard, back when Adam was only learning how to walk, to have a second child. We felt a brother or a sister would be good for Adam, and for us, that it would somehow release the pressure cooker that the three of us had become. But it didn't happen. And then things started to turn sour between Rory and me. We started sleeping in separate beds, and before long the three of us were occupying the three bedrooms in the house.

On the night of the funeral I wasn't capable of sleeping on my own – neither of us was – and so we ended up in our old bed acting out parts we no longer knew or even recognised, a long night of emotional and physical intensity, the two of us lost in our grief, making love to a complete stranger, that's what it felt like for me, anyway.

I've seen Molly Dunne. Recently, I mean. She hasn't seen me, I've been very careful about that. What she's been through is bad enough without the added nightmare of an unstable, grieving stalker outside her house. She'd be understandably alarmed if she spotted me sitting here, spying on her. I wouldn't want to do that to her.

I watch the house from my car. I park it a few doors away, at the far side of the street. I don't stay long. I pretend I'm reading a newspaper, but actually I'm keeping a steady eye on the front windows of her house. She has the blinds down on two of the three upstairs windows. I go there at different times. The blinds are always down on the downstairs windows, even during the day. I don't know what she does in there. Watch TV, I suppose.

It's hard not to feel sorry for her. She seems to have no one. She's an attractive woman, and I've often wondered why there isn't a man in her life. Throughout her emotional scenes in the coroner's court, I could see that she was a nice person. Harmless, innocent, even insubstantial, if that can be said of a solid, living human being. But overall a decent sort, and that's what matters in the end, when it comes down to it.

I haven't told Rory I come here. He'd be utterly perplexed. And furious. He has moved on. I know it is what he has to do. Men are like that. They need to sidestep, compartmentalise their fears and anxieties, even their grief. They need to feign progress. And in most cases they can. That's the difference, I think. Men can move on. They carry their emotions more lightly. Though he still has moments. Only the other day he caught me looking through old photos of when Adam was two. He sat on the sofa and looked through those photos and he cried for over an hour.

And me, how am I coping? I'm stuck in a strange place, I guess. It'll pass. Sooner or later it'll pass. I can't go on like this forever.

The front door opens and Molly steps out into the freezing air. She is wearing a three-quarter-length navy coat and black, drainpipe denins. A red scarf is wrapped around her neck. She glances up and down the road before closing the door. As if she is checking for something. Perhaps she has a sense that I have been watching her. Perhaps the trauma of the accident and her self-imposed incarceration in her house has made her hyper-nervous. She must have sold her car, because there's been no sign of it outside the house. I suppose she feels she wouldn't be able to sit behind the wheel of a car after what happened. Not *that* car, anyway.

Molly
Monday was our sacred day, the one untouchable day in the week that Tom and I set aside for each other. Tom once used the word sacrosanct about it. That pretty much summed it up. At seven thirty he'd leave his house and twenty minutes later he'd let himself in my front door and join me in bed.

We were meant to be together the Monday that I killed Veronica Harte's son. Only that was one of those rare days that Celia's needs trumped mine. She had a cast-iron reason, so I couldn't really complain to Tom, but that didn't mean I was happy about it.

'What happened to sacrosanct?' I said, when he rang me at six that morning.

A mean remark in the circumstances, and it does bring on some guilt when I think about what happened to Celia after.

The togetherness thing I always thought we had unravelled quickly after the accident. And then Celia began her own unravelling, her physical dismantling, so even if Tom and I had managed to overcome what had happened to me, had managed to hold on to each other, it would all have fallen apart as Celia's life ebbed away in front of Tom's eyes.

I can't say it wasn't tough on Tom. He told me lots of times he no longer loved her, but I find that hard to believe. I think he still loved her, even when it seemed really strong with the two of us. So he lost his wife and he lost me, all in the space of a few months. Maybe when he gets over all this he might pick up the phone, though if I'm being honest, which I know I should be, it feels like he's gone for good. He has two children, a boy and a girl, both in their teens. It can't be easy. I could be a mother to them, that's something I've put some thought into. They need a mother, poor kids. I think I'd be good at it. Anyway, they're teenagers, so it couldn't be that hard. I could be their mum and their friend. That could work.

When Tom called to cancel that Monday, it was like someone punched me in the stomach. How would I get through the day on my own? My entire week was an arrow pointing towards Monday, and Tom. I didn't believe his excuse about Celia and the hospital. 'You shit', I remember thinking, 'you lying shit'. It threw my day completely out of kilter. I might have stayed in bed all day only I was out of ciggies, and I needed them badly, especially now that I'd been lied to and abandoned. I could have walked to the shops, it's only a ten-minute walk there and back.

I remember the first time I saw Tom texting while he was driving I was so shocked I said, 'How can you drive and text at the same time?' I couldn't figure out how you could do the two things at the one time and not drive into another car. I asked him to stop because it was making me nervous, but he just laughed and said it was easy, as long as you kept your eyes on the road. So I watched him, and I could see how careful he was, his eyes darting to the phone but staying most of the time on the road. I could see how it wasn't dangerous at all.

'I wouldn't try it if I were you', he said.

'Why not? If you can do it why can't I?'

'Because you're a crap driver, sweetheart, and I'm a good driver, that's why'.

So I can't blame Tom. He did warn me.

Anyway, that's when it happened, when I was texting Tom.

Molly steps out onto the pavement and doesn't turn either left or right. She looks at the ground as if the solution to her problems might be found in its drab greyness. Veronica watches from behind her newspaper, convinced that what Molly Dunne needs more than anything else in the world is her forgiveness. An urge that is almost too strong to resist presses her to put down the paper and get out of the car and walk up to her and simply say: 'I forgive you'. But she stays where she is because she knows she could never say it. Molly's life may have been temporarily derailed in that instant when Adam appeared in front of her car, but all the suffering that she will experience, no matter whether it lasts a lifetime or a year, will not bring back into Veronica's arms the soft warm miracle that was her beautiful son. Because even if she was not a very good mother, she loved her son with an intensity she didn't know she was capable of. That had been her son's true gift to her, the opening up within of such a deep and beautiful love. Before Adam was taken from her, she might never have known that this love was inside her, waiting to flower. It had taken his sudden, violent death to bring it out, and here it was, blooming all around her. She almost feels as if he is in the car with her, her lovely, troublesome, troubled son, watching over her and her seven-month-old unborn child.

As she watches Molly, an unbidden memory comes to her: a whispered, rasping sound in her ear as Rory poured out his hatred in the coroner's court – 'Murderous bitch, if I could strangle her and get away with it, I swear I'd do it'. She remembers the precise words, and the way they were spoken. It didn't make sense to her then, but it does now. She realises she hates Molly Dunne more than the visceral, grief-fuelled hatred Rory felt during the inquest. The hatred has been lying hidden for months. It disguised itself at varying times as shock, as grief, then sorrow and, finally, pity. Pity for the woman who killed her son. If it were ever discovered that Molly Dunne was at fault for Adam's death, she would find some way to cause her grievous harm. She would not try to stop herself, it would be something she would have to do. It would be beyond her control.

It is a chilling thought, the clearest and the truest she has had since Adam was run over.

Molly lifts her eyes from the pavement and looks into the eyes of Adam's mother. She didn't know she was there, sitting in her car, watching her, but she cannot deny that there was some powerful force acting on her consciousness that caused her to look up at just the moment that Veronica Harte is realising that she is capable of a truly violent act. Veronica's expression is ambiguous. It doesn't reveal what is crystallising in her brain. It is, to Molly, a look of sadness, perhaps, even, of pity. Without thinking about what she is doing, she raises her arm and holds up her hand. It isn't a wave – it cannot be a wave – it is nothing more than an acknowledgement that the boy's mother is there and may want to talk. Veronica, as if in a trance, lifts her own hand in response.

Only a Conversation Away

'Have you ever loved me?'

It is the conversation he has been careful to avoid.

'It's not as simple as that', he says.

A careless reply and he knows it. Instead of closing the door to her doubt, it opens it a little more.

'Actually John, when you think about it, it *is* that simple'.

She is standing at the window with her back to the bed. She sees Nuala at the far side of the road, halfway down the hill. In a couple of minutes, the doorbell will ring and her chance will be lost.

'Have you ever loved me?'

Nuala is pushing open the front gate by the time a reply comes. She has been staring at him for over a minute and his body language has already provided her answer.

'The last thing I want, Evelyn, is to hurt you in any way'.

Evelyn crosses the room and walks out onto the landing. She stops at the top of the stairs and waits for the doorbell to ring. The air feels as if it has been sucked out of her lungs. She expected the truth to come at her head-on, to smack her in the face with the blunt force of its meaning; instead, it had been crouching in the long grass all along, waiting for its moment of release.

The doorbell rings and she descends the stairs and walks across the hall towards the front door.

Upstairs, John has buried his face in his hands. He had searched for a formulation of words that would liberate both of them from the nightmare that he had brought upon them, that would set them free from the captivity of their stunted relationship. He had failed to find those words, instead landing on a phrase that would satisfy no one. As soon as they were out of his mouth he wished he could retrieve them. He wanted to call out to her as she stood at the top of the stairs, he wanted desperately to get her back in the bedroom, to halt whatever he had set in motion. Instead, a familiar, crippling sense of inadequacy has turned his wishes into a state of emotional paralysis.

He lies back in the bed and stares at the ceiling, only vaguely aware of Nuala's cheery voice as she makes her way through the hall and into the kitchen.

The day has passed. Nuala has been and gone, none the wiser. It wasn't easy, concealing the effects of what had been at long last confirmed to her in the bedroom earlier, but she has always been able to find the inner strength when it was needed. Of course, Nuala sensed something, cute bitch that she is, never one to miss a trick, always alert to any sniff of drama, of family conflict. Evelyn doesn't like Nuala. What's more, she is certain that the feeling is reciprocated. But they are sisters, and while they are permitted to dislike each other, they are not afforded the luxury – for that is what it would be, a truly luxurious feeling – of not loving each other. Perhaps she should not speak for Nuala in this regard; for herself, for Evelyn, there is no escaping the fact: she loves her sister, she will always love her sister.

While they were in the kitchen, she thought she heard John quietly descending the stairs and letting himself out the front door. She couldn't let on to Nuala that anything was the matter, especially what *was* the matter, because to open the door to her spiteful commentary would have split her head in two. In any case, she has gone home.

She is lying on her bed, their bed. In the dark. She had been asleep, but she has been woken by the sound of voices drifting up the stairs from the kitchen. As a child, she was always comforted by this sound, the ebb and flow of conversation, laughter, even a raised voice, life going on beneath her as she lay on her back in the narrow single bed at the top of the house. Voices rising up through the floors and the open doors, heard from the warmth and security of her bed. Sounds she would take to the grave with her. Like now, the muffled voices of John and Emma down in the kitchen, just about reaching her ears.

She has been asking herself why she needed to know; or rather, why she needed it confirmed, for in truth she had known for a long time. She had never suspected him of cheating on her, that had never been the issue. The issue was love, or the paucity of it, sometimes the complete lack of it. She suspected early on that he was in fact incapable of love as she understood and experienced it. It had come as a shock to her, and a part of her never fully accepted it. She had loved him from the outset, and he led her to believe he loved her with equal if not greater intensity. Looking back now with the benefit of hindsight it was clear that he had persuaded himself that he loved her. She guessed it had its origin in his lack of emotional maturity, but she was no psychologist and in truth she just didn't know.

They had managed. He was out a lot, at work and at the local GAA club. They had children. Life took over, as it does. The years slipped by. But all through those busy years, Evelyn accepted now, her mind had been troubled by an absence of love in her marriage. It simmered away inside her until it eventually reached a point where she felt her head was going to explode if she didn't confront him, force an honest answer out of him. His puzzling behaviour over recent months, and his further detachment from her, had pushed her into a corner: she simply had to find out what was going on inside his head.

Now that she has released the pressure valve, she wonders what she has achieved. She is reaching the conclusion that she may have unwittingly ended their fifteen-year marriage. This, she realises with a growing sense of panic, was never the intended outcome.

Downstairs, John sits at the kitchen table. A paralysis has come over him. His easy-going ways and mannerisms, assembled over time to help him cope with a life suffused with uncertainty and insecurity, have deserted him. He doesn't know what to do next, how to proceed through the mess that he has created. He is not equipped to deal with something so emotionally charged, so significant. He can feel himself unravelling.

'Dad, what's *wrong*?'

Emma, seated across from him, has asked for the third time.

He turns his head slowly and opens his mouth to speak, but there are no words that he can find to explain what is happening. He can feel his eyes filling up with tears.

Emma has always relied on her father to lift her out of the odd moods she gets in. Now he seems a broken man. She reaches across the table and takes his hand in hers.

'I'm going to see how mum is', she says, but holds on to his tightening hand as his shoulders begin to shake and tears roll down his cheeks. She holds on through much of the sobbing, and when the worst seems to be over, she gently lets go of his hand and goes upstairs.

She is pushing open the bedroom door when her mother says from the darkness, 'Don't switch on the light'.

'Are you alright, Mum?'

'I'm fine. Tell your father to come up and see me'.

'He's in the kitchen crying. What's going on?'

'Nothing that can't be mended. Go down and tell him to come up. I need to talk to him'.

A minute later, John's tall, black shadow appears in the doorway. The light on the landing is on, the bedroom remains in darkness.

'Come in love and shut the door. Come over to the bed and hold my hand'.

The street light outside Moody's shop casts a dim orange light into the room. John sits on the bed and takes Evelyn's outstretched hand.

'I've been a bit of a fool', she begins. 'I need you to know that it doesn't matter how much or how little you love me. I know you love me in your own way, and that's good enough for me. I've no right to ask you to give more than you are able. Promise me, please, forget what happened earlier. I'll never ask you that again. I'm so sorry, love. I was feeling vulnerable, that's all. I'm over it now'.

In recent months, with the weight of guilt getting heavier and heavier, John has been experiencing what can best be described as out-of-body sensations. He went through something similar when he was a child. He never told anyone about it but the memory of that confusing, frightening experience has remained with him all through the years. He is back there now, in that same unsettling place. He looks in on the bedroom scene, as if he is merely an observer, and sees two tragic figures, worn down and dismayed, advancing towards middle age, struggling to accept the disappointments that have blighted their marriage, incapable of expressing the unspoken longings that have suddenly, shockingly, emerged into full, blinding view.

He knows he no longer has it in him to pretend. He had known from day one, but it had suited him to bury it. His tears downstairs were tears of acceptance that all had finally unravelled. He cannot put the pieces back together again. He sits on the bed, holding Evelyn's warm hand, and the only thing on his mind is Nuala, and how on earth Evelyn will take the news. She has brought it on herself, he can see that, prodding and pushing for a declaration he cannot make. Yet she doesn't deserve what it is he is duty bound to tell her. He doesn't know how to begin, or when. He sits on the bed and thinks of Nuala, and the life together the two of them have talked about. It is only a conversation away now. Only a conversation and it will all be over.

THE CALLER

Mr McEvitt wasn't accustomed to answering the doorbell on his own, so when a short ring sounded in the hallway five minutes after his wife had left for the shops, he wasn't sure if he would answer it.

Mr McEvitt was retired and lived with his wife in a suburb of Leeds. It was a typical three-bedroomed terraced house built in the 1950s with a small garden out front and a narrow garden at the back. The house was in the middle of a long straight road and the back garden mirrored an identical garden and house behind theirs. There were four large estates side by side, all with roads and avenues and parks and drives and closes and the occasional cul-de-sac. The shops to which Mrs McEvitt had walked were fifteen minutes away. The McEvitts didn't have many callers.

'Good morning, Mr McEvitt. Your wife said you'd be in, and that this would be a good time to call'.

Before he had opened the door, he had drawn the small security chain across, just in case. They were in the habit of doing this if the doorbell rang unexpectedly during the day, even if both of them were in. They also drew the chain across before they went to bed every night. It added that extra bit of security, of reassurance, though really they knew that the chain could quite easily be broken by anyone who had a mind to.

Only last week, he had heard voices in the back garden, and when he looked out the kitchen window he had seen two men in dark green overalls standing with hedge clippers in their hands at the end of the garden. They were still there when he heard his wife's key in the front door, but when he turned away from the window to call to her, to ask her why she hadn't told him there were men coming to cut the hedge, they went and disappeared. He'd called her a silly old fool when she'd said there had been no men in the garden, that he'd had another of his imaginings, the term that young doctor Sweeney had coined when they'd gone to see him before Christmas. Dr Sweeney had explained that these alarmingly real and frequently distressing daydreams were a specific and rare symptom of acute anxiety, particularly among those suffering from delayed post-traumatic stress syndrome. Never mind that trendy young doctor, he told his wife. The men had been in the garden, he had seen them.

'I'm sorry, but we're not expecting any callers', Mr McEvitt called out to the well-dressed, clean-shaven young man who was standing on the doorstep, some sort of brochure or catalogue in his left hand.

'Mrs McEvitt said you'd be more than happy to let me show you these', and his fingers flicked through the pages of the brochure he was holding.

'Where did you say you met my wife?'

'On her way to the shops. We had a grand chat altogether. Lovely woman, your wife, Mr McEvitt. She insisted I come straight here and show you these'. Again, he flicked through the glossy pages with his fingers.

'Well, I suppose there can't be any harm in it', Mr McEvitt said, and he slid the chain across and opened the door wide. The young man smiled and held out his hand. Mr McEvitt was obliged to extend his own, even though he was not in the habit of shaking hands with complete strangers.

'Nick Conway. Very pleased to meet you, Mr McEvitt'.

Mr McEvitt led the young man into the front room. As he did so, an uneasy feeling came over him.

'Mr Conway, my wife is an unusually shy woman. I can't for the life of me picture her chatting away to a complete stranger out on the street'.

'Well, to be honest, Mr McEvitt, I was the one doing most of the chatting. Your wife did indeed strike me as being unusually shy'.

Calmly, the young man placed his brochure on the coffee table beside the fireplace and, almost in the same movement, he drew a knife from an inside pocket and casually held the long, sharp blade in the air.

'No need to be alarmed, knives are only dangerous when they're in the wrong hands'.

In his prime, Mr McEvitt had been a strong, burly figure of a man, someone a robber would think twice about confronting. He knew how to handle himself, too, having spent half his working life in the army. Now in his late-seventies, his finely-toned muscles had wasted, his frame had shrunk, and he looked, and was, old and frail. He felt disorientated, staring across the single metre of space into the cold blue eyes of the stranger who was holding a knife in the air as if he might wield it any minute. He felt his dodgy leg going from under him.

'Pick yourself up and sit down on the armchair and stop playing the namby-pamby with me. Ex-army men don't fall down at the sight of a knife, do they Mr McEvitt?'

Lying helplessly on his side on the carpeted floor, Mr McEvitt could only hold one thought in his head.

'Where is my wife? What have you done to my wife?'

'I expect she'll be in the butchers or The Shopping Basket. She'll be home in half an hour. Then we can get down to business'.

'What do you want?' Mr McEvitt asked. His ribs hurt, and his right arm felt odd when he tried to move it.

'Be a wise old man and behave', Nick Conway said. 'I'm going into the kitchen to make myself a cup of tea'.

Before he left the room, he went over to the window and pulled the curtains closed.

'No funny business, right?'

With great difficulty, Mr McEvitt got to his feet and made his way to the armchair. The fall, and the trauma of what had just occurred, had left him breathless. He closed his eyes and tried to collect his thoughts. There was no point in calling out for help, which he would have done even though he had been warned not to, but his voice was weak and anyway there'd be no one in either of the next door houses at this time of the day. He would open one of the windows and call for help, except the windows were locked and needed a special key to open them.

Rita knew where the key was. She would be home shortly. What would happen then? He could hear the young ruffian in the kitchen, opening cupboards.

'What do you want?' Mr McEvitt called out. 'If it's money you're after, we don't keep any in the house. My wife will have spent most of the money she had in her purse in the shops. You'll be getting yourself into an awful lot of trouble all for the sake of the few pounds she'll have. If you go now, if you leave quietly before my wife comes home, I won't say a word about what's happened. There'll be no need for her to find out. In fact, it would be for the best if she didn't know. She's quite a worrier, my wife'.

The kettle boiled and he could hear water being poured into a cup or a mug. There came no response to what he had said.

'What do you say, Mr Conway? How's about we pretend all this never happened? You leave now, take anything you like. There's a Wedgwood vase in here that must be worth several hundred pounds. We got it as a wedding present. Why don't you take that? Before my wife comes home?'

He heard footsteps on the stairs.

'You can take my wife's jewellery', he called up after Conway. 'She keeps all her jewellery in a drawer in the bedroom. Can you hear me, Mr Conway?'

He forced himself out of the armchair. A sharp pain shot through his ribcage. He felt dizzy, but the dizziness didn't supplant the fear that had gripped him. There had been a cold, ruthless air about the young man when he had produced his knife.

He made his way towards the living room door.

'Going somewhere?'

Conway stood in the hallway.

'I didn't hear you come down the stairs', Mr McEvitt said.

'That's because I specialise in moving around quietly when I need to. Back to the armchair'.

'But what are you waiting for my wife for? What do you want with us? We're an old couple living alone with no money. We can't be of any use to you'.

'That's where you're wrong. Now go back to your armchair and wait for your wife. I'll be upstairs getting things ready'.

'What do you mean, getting things ready? Getting things ready for what?'

'Your armchair, Mr McEvitt. I don't want to have to ask you again'.

'I think I've damaged my ribcage'.

'No doubt you have. Armchair. Now'.

Reluctantly, Mr McEvitt shuffled back into the front room and lowered himself into the chair. He could hear Conway moving about upstairs. He was in the back bedroom. From the sound of it, he was moving furniture around.

An image of a terraced house near the Falls Road in Belfast came to him. He had been a captain in the Specials, and he and six of his men were searching a house for arms and explosives. He and Corporal Harding were downstairs with the husband and wife and their four children, none of them yet teenagers. A young, working-class Catholic family. The banging and the thudding of furniture being upended upstairs shook the flimsy house. He could still see the look of defiance and hatred in the eyes of the parents, and the fear in those of the children. Several times a week they raided a house just like that, leaving it a total shambles when they left, almost always empty-handed. Frequently, they smashed ornaments and pictures for the hell of it. 'Learn to cooperate with the armed forces and this kind of thing won't happen' were Captain McEvitt's parting words always, before the troops bundled themselves out the front door and climbed into their armoured trucks.

The sound of the key in the front door jolted him back to the present. In a desperate bid to get to Rita before she entered the hall, he dragged himself to his feet. He was wheezing, out of breath, and he thought he heard Conway on the stairs. He was about to call out to Rita, to tell her not to come in, under any circumstances, but everything was moving too fast for his brain and before he knew it, his wife was in the hall, the front door was closed, and there was no sign of Conway.

'Where's he gone?'

'Where's who gone, dear?'

'Conway. He has a knife'.

'Who's Conway? What knife?'

'Bloody hell, Rita, the man you met, he came to the house. I let him in because he said you told him to call. Turns out he wasn't selling anything. He had a knife. He was upstairs a minute ago, moving the furniture around. He said he was upstairs getting things ready'.

Mrs McEvitt's eyes filled with tears.

'Come on in to the kitchen and sit down and we'll have a cup of tea and work this out. I'm going to have to take you to the shops with me from now on. We can't have you in the house on your own if you're going to be imagining all kinds of horrible things. It'll be the death of you. Where on earth do these peculiar ideas come from?'

She led him into the kitchen and pulled a chair out from the table for him to sit on while she went to fill the still warm kettle.

THE MAN WITH NO NAME

He turns up at the garda station in Boyle and tells the sergeant that he is confused. The sergeant asks him, what is your name and how are you confused? To the first question he answers, I don't know, and to the second he simply says, wouldn't you be confused if you couldn't remember your name? The sergeant asks him if he has any ID. What's ID, he asks. ID is short for identification, the sergeant says. Do you have any identification on you like a passport or a driving licence or anything that says who you are? The man says if I had ID I would know who I am and if I knew who I was I wouldn't need ID. Are you taking the mickey, the sergeant asks, but he knows straight away from the bewildered look on the man's face that he isn't, that he really doesn't know who he is. Have you any items on your person that might assist us in determining your identity, the sergeant asks. The reply is in keeping with what has gone on before: I have nothing on my person, not a single thing, just the clothes I am dressed in, that's all. The sergeant remarks that it's a queer day this is going to be if this nutcase is any indication, except, of course, he doesn't say this out loud, he says it quietly to himself.

An hour passes and cups of tea are drunk and a crossword is examined, but nothing written in it. The phone rings and wakes everyone up with news of an incident on Main Street involving an elderly woman and a Latvian man who she's accused of trying to rob her handbag. Garda Burke and Garda Curtin are dispatched to the scene, to return ten minutes later saying it was only Mrs Carmody throwing a wobbly. The Latvian turned out not to be Latvian at all, but German and he wasn't asking for directions either. Why, says Garda Burke, would Frank Luthen be asking for directions and him living a mile outside the town for the past fifteen years and knowing practically everyone there is to know? Sure isn't it Frank Luthen who makes the goat's cheese and who sells it at the farmers' market every Saturday, says Garda Curtin. Why would Frank Luthen be looking for directions? According to Frank, says Garda Burke, he was handing out flyers advertising his cheese and he was attempting to hand one to Mrs Carmody when the old bag (Garda Burke's precise phrase) handbagged him outside the newsagents and accused him of being a Latvian. The sergeant says Mrs Carmody is well known for her unsavoury views and tells the two gardaí they should have arrested her for a clear-cut case of anti-Latvianism. The man who has no ID and no name watches all this carry on from his peculiar vantage point of not knowing who he is. Within an hour he knows enough to consider the town of Boyle a daft place and where daft things are duty bound to happen. Silently he hopes that if his memory does return he won't discover he's a native of the place.

A young Garda fresh out of training college is giving the man's jacket a thorough examination. He had taken it off because it was too hot and humid in the station. Sergeant, she calls, I've found something in the lining. She goes to a drawer in the main office and takes from it a small scissors. Deftly she slits the lining and withdraws from the interior of the jacket a pocket size red plastic cardholder. Inside there are two London Underground cards. The first is a laminated card with a passport size photo of a much younger man, the one who has lost his name and his identity. Here is proof that he existed on the London Underground when he was a young man, and here in the facing flap of the red cardholder is an off-peak Travelcard to the value of £2.30 and dated Thursday 26 June 1973. Sarge, she says, why would he have a London Underground Travelcard from 1973 inside the lining of his jacket? The sergeant is having a bad day and can offer no easy answers to the riddle posed. Why don't you see if any of it gets his memory going, is the best he can manage. He goes back to the phone where a furious Frank Luthen is on the line fumigating about being called a Latvian. The sergeant leans his head into his left palm and closes his eyes and holds the receiver well away from his right ear.

Sir, does this prompt your memory? The man who has forgotten who he is looks at the photo and the travel pass. Who's that, he asks the incredulous guard. It's yourself as a young man, she tells him. The man ponders this for some time then asks to see a mirror. Now in all the years in Boyle Garda Station no one has ever asked to see a mirror. Why do you want a mirror, Sir, the guard asks, to which the sergeant who has given up on Frank Luthen or perhaps the other way around, says sure the poor eejit doesn't know what he looks like, he's forgotten that too. Get the man a mirror, will you? Somehow miraculously a mirror that isn't attached to a bathroom wall is found and brought to the man. He looks at himself for a long time before declaring, that must be me so, not a bad looking specimen. And that's me how many years ago? Thirty-four, declares the guard. By the hokey, the man says, amazed that the face peering back at him in the mirrored glass is himself. He gets up from his chair and stretches. The Travelcard is in his right hand, the mirror in his left. I'm going for a walk with these and I'm going to sit on the bridge I saw earlier and think as hard as I can, he says. Go with the man and see that he comes to no harm, the sergeant says to the guard.

It is a warm sunny day in the town of Boyle. What's up that direction, the man asks the guard. Sir, that's the famous Boyle Abbey. Lough Key is up that way, too, and the road to Sligo, and Dublin if you take a right at the roundabout. I don't know what way to go, the man says. I thought you said you wanted to sit on the bridge and think, says the guard. So I did and isn't it a good job the sergeant sent you with me. What's your name, he asks. The guard tells him her name is Bríd, spelt B.R.I.D. with a fada over the I. Well you'd better call me something if I'm to call you Bríd, says the man who doesn't know who he is. Bríd blushes and says, I don't think that would be appropriate, you could after all be a wanted criminal. The man laughs out loud though inwardly the word daft floats across his brain. Who's the most notorious criminal you can think of, he asks her. Again she blushes for Bríd is a shy young woman, she will be a good cop, well able to do her job, not afraid of anything, but she'll never be comfortable in this kind of off-the-wall one-to-one encounter. Al Capone, she says eventually. Call me Al, he says. I couldn't, Sir. You could, Bríd, and you must. Here I am old enough to be your father with no name, no identity, no memory, the least you can do is give me a name until I find my old one. So say to me: will we walk to the bridge, Al? Poor Bríd, she could throttle the sergeant for sending her on this assignment, but now that she's on it she may as well go with the flow. The bridge is this way, Al, is what she says.

They walk along Patrick Street. Al comments that several of the shops are unoccupied and that the street has a rundown feel to it. The economic boom passed Boyle by and now the recession is driving the crippled town to an early grave, Bríd says. This prompts Al to ask, what economic boom? So Brid informs him that Ireland became very wealthy very quickly, that there were loads of billionaires and thousands of millionaires, that ten percent of the population for a while back was made up of foreign nationals, that Dublin went pure crazy, that for a few years everyone was making a bundle of money but not the guards, only some of them and they were crooked. After that Bríd takes a long inward breath because all the words spilled out of her in one big surprising gush. The man asks what a foreign national is, and Bríd explains it's all them people from the EU, all the Poles and Latvians and Lithuanians, all the Romanians and Hungarians and Nigerians. Al wants to know why Poles and Romanians and Nigerians would be bothered coming to a place like Boyle, so Bríd tells him they came to take all our jobs and that they all worked for less than the minimum wage but now there's no jobs, so half of them have gone back to wherever they came from and the other half are on social welfare. Here Bríd takes a short breather. She doesn't know what has come over her. Never in her life has she spoken to anyone, let alone a complete stranger, in the way that she's speaking now. It's like she can't stop now that she's started. If you ask me, she says, there's going to be trouble down the line now that the economy has upped and died on us all. Once upon a time Al might have said, do you not remember all those millions of poor unfortunate Irish men and women heading off long ago to look for work in England and America? But Al doesn't say any of this because his memory has packed its bags and gone away on a very long one-way trip itself.

They have arrived at the bridge and Bríd is talking to her colleague who has pulled up beside them in the patrol car. Is this the buck who has lost his memory, he asks and when Bríd nods he says, poor sod I knew a fella once who worked in a bank. He had a wife and three young kids and they lived in a nice house in the Dublin suburbs. Everything was going great until one day in the middle of a meeting with a client in his office he forgot who he was, who the client was, what he was doing there. He forgot the whole shebang. Everything he used to know he no longer knew. It was like Paul Daniels was sitting opposite him and clicked his fingers and his memory vanished as quickly as that. Where is he now, asks Bríd.

While her colleague continues the story Al walks away from them and leans over the parapet of the stone bridge. There's been a fortnight of heavy rain and the river is full of energy and movement. Al knows how that story is going to end, the one Bríd's colleague is telling. Al couldn't face that. He doesn't believe he is going to get his memory back. It feels as if it has gone for good. When he tries to think about his life there is nothing there. He has general knowledge but even that is sketchy. He knows there is a country called England and another called America but he cannot picture anything about them, even though he thinks he may have lived in both. He cannot remember where he was yesterday or for how long he has been wandering. Why or how he has ended up in Boyle is a mystery to add to the mystery of his life. Bríd walks to where he is leaning over the parapet, the squad car having sped off to the chipper, where the sergeant's fresh cod and chips await collection. Ah you're back, he says turning to face her. He puts his arms around her because it is such a simple thing to do. He would like Bríd to return the hug, but there's little chance of that happening. When to hug and when not to hug is not in the rulebook. All she can do is stand with her arms by her side in the middle of banjaxed Boyle while some strange sad man wraps his arms around her as if she is his mother. For months now she has been wondering why she joined the force. She thought it would be one thing, but it's more like a thousand-and-one things, none of which make sense. There, there, Al, she says not knowing what else to say and she throws the rulebook out and puts her arms around the man with no name and says again, there, there, Al, everything will be alright.

CARLOW

Lincoln's hands were what she had noticed the first time she'd laid eyes on him. She and Joe were only moved in when a knock on the open back door brought her down the stairs and in through the kitchen. She was wearing tight-fitting jeans and an orange t-shirt that clung to her breasts. She became aware of how she must have looked when she saw the stranger's eyes roam freely and without shame or embarrassment all over her. He'd kept that look well hidden ever since.

'Just thought I'd welcome ye to the parish', he'd said in a coarse voice destroyed by twenty years on the fags. The clean jeans and the ironed shirt, the lighted roll-up that hung off his lower lip, the elegant hands – these were the things she remembered most about that first meeting. He'd said hello, is the man of the house around at all? And when she'd led him round to the front of the house to where Joe was busy cutting back the overgrown hedge of hawthorn and alder, he'd introduced himself.

'I'm Lincoln Savage. I'm over the hill'.

He smiled as he caught them glancing at each other.

'Literally over the hill', and he raised his arm and pointed towards the hill behind the house.

They'd gone inside and Mairéad had made tea. Joe took down a couple of plain wooden chairs that were turned upside down on the kitchen table. Lincoln remained standing, placing his backside against the unlit range in a manner that betrayed long familiarity with the once always-warm stove; in its own subtle way, his casualness seemed to Mairéad to insinuate some sort of tribal possession of the room. He appeared completely at ease as he rolled one cigarette after another with his immaculately-groomed fingers, his clear blue eyes coming to rest on Joe's open, friendly face, and occasionally, though not often, on that of Mairéad. There was something edgy and unpredictable about his demeanour that both appealed to and repelled her. She caught herself staring at him in a way that she had never stared at anyone. He intrigued her. Perhaps the clean, pressed jeans and crisp blue shirt were a deliberate attempt to camouflage this edginess, this thinly-disguised volatility. Joe, she knew well, would see none of this in him. Joe only saw surfaces in people; he wasn't literate in the language of interiors.

She liked Lincoln Savage's slimness, and his long legs, and above all, she liked his hands. Several times she caught herself staring at his fingers as they nimbly rolled another cigarette. Four cigarettes he'd smoked in the space of an hour that summer afternoon. She had never in her life been so struck by a man's physicality as she was by his intense presence. It took her completely by surprise. Until that afternoon, she would not have thought of herself as a sexual person. She had had sex only with Joe, and she had taken pleasure in at least some of these intimate exchanges, though of late the whole messy business had become a chore, something that had to be engaged in, because that's what married couples do.

She hoped he hadn't noticed her staring at Lincoln. She hoped even more that Lincoln hadn't, though she suspected he had. He seemed the type who would notice such things. Was this what they called pure physical sexual attraction? Whatever it was, it frightened her, for she knew intuitively that it would be too strong for her to resist were the situation to present itself.

As the weeks passed, however, it became clear that Lincoln was only interested in Joe. Joe was the archetypal outdoor man. He'd grown up on a farm, studied horticulture at college, worked for a few years with a large landscaping contractor, before setting up on his own eight years ago. He was naturally strong and could stay on his feet from morning till night without breaking sweat. He worked within a radius of fifty kilometres and was kept busy all year. Everything he had – the van, the trailer, the high-quality machine tools, the rotovator, the strimmers, the mowers – he owned outright. He led a simple life that was dominated by work, and by the slowly-stagnating marriage to Mairéad.

Lincoln took to Joe and Joe to Lincoln because they suited each other, temperamentally and practically. Lincoln, like Joe, spent his days out in the open; erecting and mending fences, digging and clearing drains, cutting and pruning hedges, tending his cattle and his sheep. He became a regular caller to Joe and Mairéad's, though it didn't take her long to notice that he rarely landed if Joe was not around. The two men struck up an easy friendship, one that excluded Mairéad. Joe lent Lincoln the rotary mower, the chainsaw, the strimmer with the hedge-cutting attachment. In return, Lincoln, who had a magician's touch with machinery, fixed whatever needed fixing. This aspect of Lincoln's life intrigued Mairéad, for Lincoln's fingernails and his hands were always impeccably clean. Joe was not a dirty person, but he could let a couple of days go by between hot showers and think nothing of it. By contrast, she imagined Lincoln in his shower every morning without fail, probably every evening, too. He was that clean. He smelt that fresh.

In July of the following year, Joe and Lincoln went off together to the National Ploughing Championships. They left at six in the morning, promising to be home before dark. Mairéad was glad to see Joe happy. Things had run aground at home, in the bedroom specifically, with Joe claiming exhaustion and Mairéad drawing on her usual store of excuses whenever Joe was in the mood, which wasn't often. She waved the two of them off, having cooked them a dawn breakfast.

It was long past dark when Joe called her. He sounded pissed.

'We're staying with one of Lincoln's cousins', he shouted into the phone. There were voices in the background. She heard women's laughter.

'Are you not working in Clancy's all day tomorrow?'

'I am, I am. I'll be home by eight. Gotta go, bye'.

She cooked up a fry, assuming Joe would invite Lincoln in, but the fry died a slow death in the oven. She tried phoning his mobile, but it was turned off.

Just after one, Joe's van pulled in to the driveway. He was alone.

'Jesus, where were you? I was sure you'd had an accident'.

She had never seen him look so pale, so exhausted. He reached out with his right arm and propped himself against the frame of the door. His head dropped and he stood without moving a muscle for half a minute.

'Tom Clancy rang', she said.

'If he rings again, tell him the van broke down'.

He slept through the afternoon and into the evening. At nine he surfaced, made a pot of tea, buttered four slices of bread and went back up to the bedroom to watch TV.

When Mairéad came to bed an hour later, he was asleep, and when she woke early the following morning, he was already up and gone. He came home late that evening, complaining of a sore throat and a temperature. She could see he was in no mood to talk, but there were things she wanted to know.

'So, how was Carlow?'

'The whole town was drunk as far as I could see'.

'You were well on when you rang me'.

'Was I? I can't remember'.

'What are Lincoln's cousins like?

'I didn't meet any of his cousins'.

'But you said you were staying with one of his cousins. You told me that on the phone'.

He shifted position, looked out the window, avoiding her steady gaze.

'I don't know why I said that. It was his sister we were with'.

'I never heard him mention his sister'.

'Yeh, well, you know what he's like, he's cagey, he only tells you what he wants to tell you'.

'Why would he keep his sister a secret?'

'Beats me'.

'What's she like? Does she look at all like Lincoln? Is she married?'

'Jesus, Mairéad what's with all the fucking questions?'

'I'm just curious. We haven't spoken since you got home'.

'I haven't been well'.

'Even so. You've been doing your level best to avoid me'.

'That's a ridiculous thing to say. I had jobs to do'.

'I'm not stupid, Joe'.

'Who ever said you were stupid?'

'So, where did you end up sleeping?'

He turned his head and glowered at her. 'Honestly I can't fucking remember'.

'Why are you being like this?'

'Like what, for fuck's sake?'

'Was Lincoln as drunk as you?'

'Lincoln could drink Shane McGowan under the table'.

'Were there women there, apart from Lincoln's sister?'

'The pub was crawling with them. And they were all asking for it'.

She stared at him. He was like a stranger standing in front of her.

'You must remember waking up', she said.

He wouldn't meet her gaze, choosing instead to stare out the window.

'I'm not able for this crap', he said at last, and he walked out of the room and climbed the stairs.

She remained in the armchair for a long time, unaware of the slow retreat of the light of the day from the room. Later, in the silence and darkness of the house, she drifted off to sleep where she sat.

Lincoln stood warming his arse against the range. It was where he always stood when he came to call. Outside, under the dark November sky, the rain was coming down in great sweeping gusts.

'Joe told me the fox nearly got in to the barn the other night. Ye were lucky to have heard the hens'.

'When were you talking to Joe?'

'He dropped by on his way to the garden centre. He said the fox would have killed the lot if you hadn't heard them'.

'They were making an awful racket'.

'Isn't it a good job you're a light sleeper', he said. 'Joe would sleep through an earthquake'.

He had taken his tobacco out of his jacket pocket and was halfway through rolling a cigarette.

'I don't understand why Joe was over at your place', she said. 'When he left here he said he was running late'.

Lincoln frowned and tilted his head slightly and gave her a curious look. He didn't appear in the least perturbed by the turn in the conversation. It was her face, not his, that reddened. She had suspected for several months – since the Carlow incident, in fact – but the notion was so outlandish, so utterly laughable, that whenever she thought she might say something to Joe, she gasped at her own stupidity, at her newly-discovered ability to consider the impossible possible. But sometimes when she was making the bed, or when she was peeling potatoes or chopping an onion, or when she was out in the vegetable plot doing a bit of weeding, her suspicions came over her like a tidal wave and engulfed her. When this happened, she had no doubts. She saw the two of them in Lincoln's barn, or wedged behind his half-open back door, or on the landing, Lincoln's long hands bringing Joe to a sweet, silent climax. She even imagined them kissing, long sensual kisses as the hot water of Lincoln's shower cleansed their naked, exhausted bodies.

Following these visions, she would be dizzy and disorientated and she would have to go upstairs and lie down on the bed and close her eyes and force her mind away from the torrent of suspicions that were running wild inside her head. Now, in the kitchen, alone with Lincoln, she was bringing the horror out into the open. She hadn't planned to, but she was already launched and she didn't think she would be able to stop.

'You look like you've just been caught halfway up a ladder with no knickers on', Lincoln said. He had his back to the warm range. His eyes penetrated her skull. 'You think me and Joe are up to some funny business, don't you? You think he comes over the hill for more than a chat and a fixing of the strimmer'.

Her cheeks were burning now.

'I think the time has come for me to dispel those suspicions', he said.

He seemed to glide across the kitchen tiles towards her.

After their lovemaking, which was awkward and unpleasant, she made him a cup of tea and he drank it at his usual place.

'Do you think Joe will suspect?' he asked.

'You and me doing what we've just done is probably the last thing Joe would suspect. He trusts me, and he thinks the world of you'.

'It will be better the next time. You won't be as tense', he said.

Mairéad looked at his hands as he rolled a cigarette. They were no longer a thing of beauty to her. They had, in the space of a confusing hour, become an extension of Lincoln's detached personality. The hands, soft as they were, had been cold and unfeeling as they moved over her. The long, elegant fingers found their way effortlessly, but they lacked sensuality inside her. They switched her off instead of on.

She knew nothing about him. That which she thought she knew lay in ruins. There was no longer any physical attraction on her part; something closer to revulsion inhabited that space inside her now. She had no idea how he would take the rebuttal. Neither did she know how the three of them would manage from now on. A new notion, that he had seduced her in order to put her off the scent, was beginning to make her dizzy all over again. Only one thing was certain: it was the last time Lincoln Savage would lean his cute arse against her range. She steeled herself to tell him how it was going to be between the three of them from now on.

WHO KNOWS BERNARD ASHE?

I have always been a loner, preferring my own company to that of others. I've made my bed and am happy to lie on it. Alone, of course. There are many things that I am loathe to share, and my bed is one of them.

I live near Porte d'Auteuil, on the top floor of a five-storey, late nineteenth-century house. As Parisian houses go, it is relatively modest, yet it has a certain clean style that I like. I don't go in for fussiness in buildings, especially interiors, so this place suits my mood just fine. The delightfully-simple stairway winds in a graceful spiral upwards, depositing dwellers at their required level, where they unlock their doors while holding in their spare hand some item or other, invariably a baguette or a plastic shopping bag from the local Mono-Prix at the end of the street, or in the case of Mr et Mme Blondin on the third floor, a delicate little cardboard box filled with half-a-dozen works of art from the exquisite patisserie off rue de Seigneur.

I know all of the residents to see and to exchange a few pleasantries, mainly about the weather. In that respect, Parisians are like people the world over, though they would not take kindly to that remark, Parisiens being of a firm belief that they are a breed apart. The couple below me I know a little better, having helped them last Christmas to find kennels for their shih-tzu. They brought me back a gift from their holidays, a factory-made miniature replica of a Dutch windmill. It was a thoughtful gesture, I'll give them that much, but I couldn't bear to have the thing in my apartment, so I buried it in the rubbish the next day.

As a postscript, their dog was run over a week after they returned, out on the street, in front of the building. Poor Clementine, she just happened to be looking out the window when she saw Lulu being chased under the wheels of a bus by a wolfhound that had broken free from its owner. Clementine was completely distraught, as anyone would be who thought her dog was in the next room. She still doesn't know how she got out of the building, and, I suppose, she never will now, unless I decide to tell her that it was I who found her downstairs in the lobby, and it was I who opened the door onto the street, if only to shut off the irritating squeaks that were piercing my ears and giving me a headache. Needless to say, I am not about to mention any of this to Clementine.

A young Englishwoman moved into one of the two second-floor apartments last March. She's a writer, or so she tells me, though she hasn't shown me any of her work, which is probably a blessing. She's working on a novel, her second. She also writes poetry, and tells me she has a collection coming out in the autumn. A small publishing house in Ireland, of all places, is publishing it. That's how we started talking, actually. She spotted me in the local boulangerie a few months ago with an *Irish Times* under my arm, which was unusual in itself, for it's rare that I bother to buy one. Julie, that's the Englishwoman's name, Julie Blackman, tapped me on the arm and said, 'you must be Irish'. Not especially original, but then everyone can't be, though one might expect something a little sharper from a writer. I fell into conversation with her, and then an extraordinary thing happened. We left the boulangerie, which is a good four hundred metres from where I live, and walked back together, neither of us knowing that the other lived in the same building. It was a decidedly odd experience, coming to the front door and both of us saying at the same time, 'This is where I live'. Since then, she's had me down to dinner three times, and I sense a fourth invitation is on the way. I had her up to my place just the once, merely to be civilised and polite and to at least be seen to be doing the right thing. I get the feeling she would like our little friendship to move into another gear, but I'm more than happy to remain in neutral.

My apartment is not a large one, but it is perfect for me. I wouldn't know what to be doing with double the space, which is what the Englishwoman has. Her place is full of clutter, incredible when one considers she has only been in situ for four months. I like to keep things simple. My furniture is modern and stylishly plain. My bookshelves have books only on them, and the proper amount. There's nothing more untidy looking than a bookcase that's also used as a receptacle for keys and candles and staplers and cameras and, in the Englishwoman's case, a place to dry your undergarments. She had three bras and three pairs of knickers pinned to the slender shelves with large plastic pegs the last evening I went down to dinner. She fumbled and blushed and removed them as soon as she saw me staring at them, but I wouldn't be at all surprised if she had left them there on purpose, as a tempter, so to speak. She obviously doesn't know Bernard Ashe.

Tomorrow, Monday, I'm back at work after a week's break. I work in a small travel agency on rue de Berri, off les Champs Elysees. It is owned and run by Mme Lefebvre, an attractive woman who celebrated what was rumoured to be her fiftieth birthday two weeks ago. She tried to keep it quiet, and she has that Parisian coolness that allows her maintain a professional distance from even her longest serving members of staff, but it was impossible not to be aware of something going on, what with the flurry of personal calls she received throughout the day, the half dozen bouquets of flowers and the dozen or more envelopes that arrived in the morning that were clearly cards and not business letters. And then at the end of the day I took an incoming call which informed me that Mme Lefebvre's limousine was outside. Without so much as a word of goodbye, she swept through the glass-fronted door and stepped into the waiting limo. Such style!

Mme Lefebvre runs a tight ship. She started up the business with her husband twenty-two years ago, out in the fashionable suburb of Malmaison, and when he dropped dead of a heart attack nine years ago she decided to move the business to the city centre. I joined shortly after she re-launched the agency in rue de Berri. Since then, I've worked diligently for Madame and she in turn has been an inspiration to work for. She handles her blue chip clients elegantly and intuitively, appearing to know exactly what they want before they know themselves, yet she manages to give them the impression that they are the ones calling the shots and making the choices. It is a gift. She is also a very fair employer, and we all five of us respect her for that. She is not the type of woman who will hand out praise, yet I know she values my diligence and my professionalism.

Despite being in the travel business I am not especially fond of travelling and I usually don't leave Paris, unless I have to return home for a funeral or a wedding. Even then, I'll try to avoid the ordeal, and only if it's pointed out to me that I have no choice will I agree to make the journey. Fortunately, no one has died for several years, and no one of any consequence has got married. I live in dread of the phone call that will summon me back. I have few warm feelings for the country or for the home that I left all those years ago. I've always been of the opinion that some people are born in the wrong place, and sometimes even at the wrong time. My parents would never be able to understand such a sentiment. I tried to explain it to them that first Christmas I returned home, having decided to settle here, but got nowhere. They belong to an old school that I do not recognise, one that expects families to stay together, one that expects siblings to carry on the traditions, and the business, if there is one. In my case, being the eldest and the only boy, and being clever, it was taken for granted that I would assume responsibilities for the management of the stud farm when my father felt it was time to step down. Even when I was in my mid-teens, the notion of taking over the business was laughable. I am not and have never been fond of horses.

They still can't come to terms with the fact that their only and gifted son is working in a travel agency, and a small one at that. I have tried to explain to them that the position I hold is of some considerable consequence, and that the agency's size is not what counts: what counts, I tell them, is the quality of service it provides, and the reputation it garners within the profession. All my parents choose to see is the small premises on the admittedly gloomy rue de Berri and that is enough for them. The last time they came to visit, over four years ago, I could see how disappointed in me they were. Bless them, they did their best to hide their feelings, but it was beyond them. Subtlety would not be their forte. I do not expect to see them in Paris again. They have always preferred to be close to their horses, and to my two sisters, both of whom are married now. They and their respective husbands have built enormous houses on my parents' land. Or so I am told. As I said, I haven't been back there for some time.

I spent my week's leave relaxing and reflecting on how well my life is going right now. I have worked hard to be where I am and I have good reason to believe that my star is in the ascendancy.

Each morning I went for a stroll in the Bois, and in the afternoons I read, sometimes at home, and sometimes at one of my favourite cafés. On the Friday, on Julie's suggestion, or rather her insistence, the two of us headed off to the Yeats exhibition which is showing in the Bibliotheque Nationale. Julie knows her Yeats and spent the best part of the morning lecturing me on the many and various aspects of that extraordinary man's life. After half-an-hour of non-stop information, however, I wished she would stop, or at least slow down, but instead she appeared to get nervous and increased her babbling until frankly I thought I was going to shout at her. I held my counsel, as this is always the best course of action. Over lunch she calmed down and we enjoyed an hour of relative peace, and then in the afternoon I was able to return the favour and do my own babbling, when we took a bus to Musee des Beaux Arts to see the Jack Yeats exhibition. The two exhibitions are a curatorial collaboration between the two cultural institutes. I have been something of a Jack Yeats aficionado since the age of twelve, when my class was taken to the National Gallery in Dublin one morning. I took to him at once and didn't bother with the rest of the old stuff on the dreary walls. Our teacher, Ms Browne, was furious with me for detaching myself from the group. She said, when I had finally been tracked down in front of *Liffey Swim*, that it had been inconsiderate of me 'in the extreme' to leave the main group and 'rude beyond belief' to the tour guide, who I'm certain didn't care one way or the other if there was one less brat in yet another party of brats.

You may gather from that last little outburst that I am not at all fond of children. I have never once regretted not having any of my own. Julie has spoken to me about children. She says children enhance and change for the better any man. How she can possibly know this is an obvious question to put to her, but I fear I would merely be encouraging her to speak on the matter even more than she has already done. I have told her that I do not like children and that, in fact, I frequently leave a room into which children enter. I have no patience for them at all, I tell her. She refuses to believe I can be so intolerant, and is convinced I would make a wonderful father.

I know what she is up to. Here she is, an impoverished writer in Paris, an expensive city that gobbles up and spits out writers by the mouthful, and here I am, a good-looking man the right side of forty, intelligent, settled, with a secure, well-paid job. I suppose I should be flattered by her interest. She is, after all, quite a beauty, but marriage is something I have never considered. Someone should have a word in her ear that she's barking up the wrong tree. Imagine me, Bernard Ashe, marrying someone like Julie Blackman. It would be laughable were it not for the fact that she has been considering it. I am convinced of it.

Julie Ashe. The name has a distinct ring to it. Much better than Blackman. But what am I thinking? The mere thought of getting hitched to Julie Blackman's chaotic life is too absurd for words. I couldn't possibly consider it.

It is Tuesday morning and I am not my usual, composed self. Two things happened to me yesterday, both unconnected, both upsetting, and both utterly perplexing. The first is the more serious, especially as it came out of the blue, well, both came out of the blue, in fact, but the first has potentially-serious consequences, whilst the second is so trivial and frankly bizarre that I am surprised how much it is troubling me.

When I arrived at work yesterday morning, after my week away, Mme Lefebvre was sitting at my desk. Beside her, sitting on my chair, was a young man, no more than twenty-five, if that. She introduced him as Patrice Laroche and announced that he would be working with me from now on. I was speechless and simply stared at the young man. He wasn't at all fazed by my standing there looking down at him; in fact he had a proprietary air about him, as if he and not I was the one who was an established presence in the office. He returned my gaze with not a trace of embarrassment or guilt, and this despite the fact that he was sitting in my chair. I was so taken aback that I managed not to utter a single word to Madame Lefebvre before she went back to her office, leaving the two of us alone together, he sitting on my chair, me standing over him. I approached *la patronne* immediately, seeking an explanation. She told me in what can only be described as a terse, impatient tone that it had been clear to her for some time that I was under performing, and that rather than let me go she was doing the honourable thing and bringing in assistance. She added that in this business second chances are rare and that I should be grateful that she was giving me an opportunity to prove myself because very few would in the circumstances. I asked her to elaborate on how I was under performing, a question which I felt bound to ask, however it quickly became apparent that the question was either misjudged, or mistimed, or both, for she then said that the fact that I was unaware that I was under performing was deeply worrying. After a sleepless night, I've come to the view that she is preparing the ground for my dismissal.

Compared with this monumental upheaval, the other thing that happened yesterday seems unimportant, yet it appears to be occupying even more of my thoughts than Mme Lefebvre's nasty manoeuvres. Indeed I am for some unknown and most peculiar reason more upset about it.

This is the thing. I arrived home from my thoroughly depressing and surreal day at the office last evening to find a one-sentence note from Julie Blackman under my door.

'I am leaving Paris straightaway', she writes, 'as I find your coldness towards me unbearable'.

What is the young woman on about? Has she gone off the rails completely? I have no idea what she is talking about. For the record, I would like to state that I have gone out of my way to be friendly and polite to her, even when, believe me, it would have been easier to be, as she put it, 'unbearably cold'. This is precisely why I value and protect my independence and my privacy. You give an inch ...

The curious aspect to this unpleasant development is that I find myself feeling sorry for her. She is clearly a fragile creature, not able for this world. She puts on a brave face, but I can now see that underneath it all she is vulnerable. Her behaviour, though, with this unwarranted, paranoid letter – honestly, it goes too far. It casts me in a poor light and is unforgivable. It just goes to show that I was right all along about her. Yet another unstable, deluded woman with notions beyond my comprehension.

I open the door of my apartment as it is time to go to work, but close it again as I can hear Julie down below. It sounded like suitcases being dragged across the landing. So, she really is moving out. On account of my 'unbearable coldness'. When I read her letter again just now, I became convinced it was a ploy on her part to draw me in. How can she accuse me of being cold towards her? I've been too friendly, that's the problem. I've a good mind to go down and tell her exactly what I think of her letter, and of her sudden departure. But that would be playing into her hands. It is what she is hoping for. I have my own hope as I lean my back against my door and wait to hear her descend the stairs, and it is this: do not, Julie, come up to say a tearful goodbye. If you do, you will find that I am not in, that I have already left for work. You will perhaps sense or even know that I am here, because you are no fool that way, but the drama, Julie Blackman, you must know that I could not bear all that drama, all that emotion.

A MOMENT OF CLARITY

He sat on the high stool and leaned his elbows on the kitchen counter and thought about what it would be like to be on his own again. One more time around the house of loneliness. He should be used to it by now, but he knew he'd never get used to the emptiness of days that would stretch effortlessly into weeks and months and which would swallow him up. Just like before.

He heard a rustle in the fireplace and slid off his stool to find out what was happening to the fire he'd lit ten minutes ago. Thank Christ, he thought, a bit of warmth on the horizon. It was bitterly cold in the damp house.

'It sounds like you're well rid of him', said Beverly, and she looked to catch the waitress's attention, a young Latvian, pretty, with rotten English and a winning smile. 'I'll have another latte', she said, when the girl arrived at the table.

'Oh, give me one, too', sighed Mary.

'I'll have a mint tea', said Bernadette, gloomily.

There were no other takers.

'If he was here now his tongue would be hanging out over that', Aine said, her eyes following the waitress as she moved among the tables.

'I don't want you all to start ganging up on him', Bernadette said. 'I know I've painted a terrible picture of him, but I'm probably being a bit unfair. He has his good points'.

'He's a bastard. Let him rot away in his damp little dungeon. It's you I'm worried about', said Beverly.

'I'll be fine', said Bernadette, inwardly recoiling from the hardness in her friend's voice.

'I'm only looking', Rob had said that first time. It was his constant line of defence.

'There's nothing wrong with looking at a beautiful woman', she'd said. 'It's the way you look that scares me'. She knew by the way he had gone silent that she had touched a nerve. 'You're infatuated with young attractive women. It's as if you've never grown up'.

'That's nonsense', he'd said.

'How would you feel if you saw me staring lustfully at a good looking, younger man? You'd be pretty pissed off, I'm sure you would'.

'I don't care who you stare at', he'd said.

'You see things that aren't there', he'd said another time. 'You see me talking to a woman and you immediately suspect I'm flirting with her. It's your problem, Bernadette, not mine'.

It had gone on like that for a long time. His refusal to accept any personal responsibility for what she saw as disloyal behaviour had become a form of cancer eating through their togetherness.

'Was Rob ever unfaithful?' Mary asked, waking Bernadette out of her thoughts.

'That's not the point. His behaviour was in itself unfaithful', said Beverly.

'Looking is one thing, doing something about it is another', Mary persisted. 'Did Rob ever, you know ...?'

'How would Bernadette know?' snapped Beverly. 'He could have slept with twenty women for all Bernadette would know'.

'How about letting her answer for herself?'

'Not as far as I know', Bernadette said.

'It wouldn't surprise me one bit if he's undressing some flighty little thing as we speak', Beverly said.

'It would surprise me', Bernadette said.

He was back on the fags. The roll-ups, not the filters, though he'd progress to those soon enough. *Coronation Street* would be on in a few minutes. He and Bernadette would often come here, to this pub that no one came to before nine in the evening, and they would sit by the open fire and talk and drink, and when *The Street* came on they'd move over with their drinks to the counter and let the storyline wash over them like a healing balm of benign familiarity. Last year, around this time, he recalled, they'd just emerged from yet another destructive bout of misunderstandings and resentment and bitter battles in the most unfailingly embarrassing places and they had rescued each other over a few precious days and nights in his house. They'd come to the pub at six every evening, where a seductive peace wrapped itself around them.

He stepped outside into the dusk, cupped his hands and lit his roll-up. An east wind blew a vicious breeze down the street, catching the left side of his face. There wasn't a sinner about. A car whizzed by, music blaring, alloy wheels shining, twenty over the speed limit. A construction truck rumbled by. All was quiet again. There were two shops in the village, and the one attached to the pub was the busiest, staying open till eleven. No one must have needed anything tonight. No one needed a drink, either. He was the only customer, and even he was standing outside.

Coronation Street was just beginning when he went back inside. He went to the bar and ordered another pint off the bored young girl who made no effort to be friendly, though he'd seen her many a time chatting away to boys and girls of her own age. I am an old man to her, he thought, and he leaned on the counter and watched the comings and goings on the screen. He wished the half-hour drama would go on forever. The characters appeared more real to him than anyone he knew.

She was worn out from the stress of it all. Now, at the end of another day without him, she sat on the edge of the bed in the eye-shadow light of the moonlit room and breathed in and out slowly, trying to calm her mind. She had a presentation to make in the morning and she realised with a weary exhaustion that she hadn't prepared a thing. She switched her bedside light on and, leaning across to the small bookcase beside her bed, pulled a book from one of the shelves. It opened where she had placed half-a-dozen photographs between the pages. They'd been taken last summer; two outside the front door of the cottage, two along the narrow back road that led to the old stone bridge over a point on the Starling River, and two in the car. She had taken three of him and he had taken three of her. It seemed apt that there were none of them together.

It was on the back road that he had asked her to marry him, the same day the photographs had been taken. There was a bend in the road, and a year-old plantation of spruce and larch on either side, and they had kissed, one of those long, gentle kisses that they seemed to specialise in, though they had never spoiled it by making reference to it. He had bought her a ring and he had removed her glove and slid the ring along her finger, and it was only then they'd noticed the dozen or so sheep eyeing them from the edge of the plantation; silent, eerie witnesses to their private pledge.

She turned off the lamp and lay on the bed and was dismayed at her stubbornness and her stupidity. She had almost lost him. He wasn't perfect, but who was? She had accused him of being a philanderer, when in truth all he had ever done was gape at pretty young women. She knew he would never have the courage to do any more than look.

Tomorrow, after the presentation, she would drive to his house. She wouldn't call in advance, she would walk in the door and tell him everything was going to be alright.

'I'd be careful if I were you. Women can be chillingly single-minded when they choose to be. They have the ability to cut you right out of their life. I've seen it. I know'.

Bernadette wouldn't behave like that. He said so to his friend, who was at the other end of the phone.

'Believe me, Rob, Bernadette is like any woman who's been wounded, or who feels she's been wronged. Don't expect any warmth or pity or compassion. If she's capable of treating you like you say she's treated you in the past, she's more than capable of carrying it through to the bitter end. My guess is she's cut you off already. I'd start thinking about moving on if I were you'.

He woke to a cloudless morning and on an impulse decided to drive to Streedagh, north of Sligo town. The last time he'd been there was the summer before last, when he and Bernadette had gone for a swim. He recalled how that day, which had begun with such promise, had ended with the two of them having a row in a restaurant in Sligo. The recollection brought a sourness with it and he brushed it aside before it had a chance to alter his mood. The conversation he'd had with his friend the previous evening remained with him and what was remarkable about it was that the feeling he had this morning was not a heavy, downcast one. During the night, lying in bed, he, too, had experienced a moment of clarity. And when he woke later after several hours of undisturbed sleep, he knew that she was gone and that she wouldn't be coming back. He was neither surprised nor regretful. It was a fact and there was nothing he could do about it. She had not only made up her mind, she had made up his.

Approaching Sligo, he felt in need of a coffee and remembered that the café he and Bernadette used to frequent and which had closed for renovations had reopened. He parked the car in Market Yard and strolled down the street towards the café. The air was crisp, the strip of sky above the buildings a bright, hard blue. He felt a lightness in his head and in his step. Walking into the café his eyes settled on the young woman who used to work there before it closed and who was this morning standing behind the counter, her bare, slender shoulders bent over the newspaper she was reading. She had been a cause of friction the last few times he and Bernadette had been here. He'd been glancing at her the entire time they had been in the café, Bernadette had said. And when the row continued into the afternoon, she'd accused him of having ulterior motives in frequenting the café.

Normally he sat at one of the tables near the window. This morning, he took a seat at the counter.

'Good morning'.

The young woman looked up from her newspaper and smiled.

'Hello', she said, closing the paper. 'Long time no see'.

'Good to see the café open again'.

'Good to have a job again'.

'I thought you'd have been snapped up by one of the other coffee shops'.

'There you go. It's their loss'.

'It *is* their loss. You make the best double espresso in town'.

'Thanks, but making a nice cup of coffee isn't my life ambition'.

It was just the two of them in the small café. He hoped no one would come in and spoil the all-too-easy one-on-one.

'What *is* your life ambition?'

She smiled and gave him a curious look that he was unable to read. He knew why Bernadette had reacted as she had. That smile. Those eyes. She wasn't warning him off, he was sure of that.

'I don't know you well enough to share that', she said.

She turned to make the coffee.

'What has you in town today?'

'I'm heading out to Streedagh for a long walk. I might go to a movie later, if there's something decent on'.

'*Source Code* just opened. It's meant to be really good', she said.

She had her back to him, waiting for the coffee to drop its last drops into his cup. He noticed she had a small tattoo in what looked like the shape of a swallow in flight at the back of her left shoulder. He hadn't noticed this before. He liked tattoos on women. Bernadette didn't have any. She was conservative in that way.

She turned and placed his coffee on the counter in front of him. The next move, if there was to be a next move, was up to him. He would bottle it, of course. That was the part that Bernadette didn't get; that all he ever did was look. He had never been unfaithful, not because of any self-imposed moral constraints, but because he had been incapable of getting beyond first base in these kinds of situations. He would sit and drink his coffee. He might even order a second. He would make idle chat until the moment had passed, as it always did. Or a customer would enter and put an end to it that way. It was now or it was not at all.

She watched him lift his cup and bring it to his lips. It was just the two of them in the café. She lived for moments like these, when the tension filled the air and she couldn't tell which way it would go. Sometimes, not very often, she took the initiative. More often than not, she let them sweat it out.

WATCHING *THE VIRGINIAN*

It is the beginning of August and it is your first day down at the beach and everything is familiar. You step on the stones and you remember how, on your last day, last summer, you tried to count all the stones on the beach. Now you look at the stones all around you and you know you would never be able to count them unless you divided the beach up into bits and did one bit every day. Even you know that's impossible, so instead of counting them, you make a guess. Ten thousand stones is the number you come up with. You are so sure of this that you are already looking forward to telling your father when he comes back from the city. You would tell your mother, but you know she wouldn't be interested. Still, you might tell her anyway.

Your mother is busy right now. She's sitting on a seat and she's talking to Mrs Grimshaw. Mrs Grimshaw is a strange person. One of her eyes is crooked. You always try to look at the good eye but no matter how hard you try you always end up staring at her crooked eye. It scares you, that eye that has a life of its own, that squints at something just to your left as her good eye pins you to the ground. When Mrs Grimshaw asks you a question, your head goes fuzzy and you get confused and you blurt out something that makes her frown. She looks so cross when she frowns. As you look at her now, you realise that you have never once seen her smile. This strikes you as odd, as your mother and your father smile a lot.

The Grimshaws live a couple of doors down from your house and some nights last year you went down there to be minded while your parents went for a walk along the prom and then for a drink in the hotel. You don't like the hotel, even during the daytime when there are other children there, but at night it's a horrible place with all the grownups drinking and smoking and making so much noise. The man who owns the hotel doesn't like children to be in the lounge at night which is why you've only been there a few times. Your parents don't go there often. They know you get nervous when they go out at night.

Last year Mrs Grimshaw gave you raspberry lemonade and left a newly-opened tin of Afternoon Tea biscuits on the dining room table and said to help yourself. That was a treat you won't forget in a hurry, because you hardly ever get lemonade at home and you never get fancy biscuits. Already you are wondering if Mrs Grimshaw has a tin waiting in the dining room for you. This makes you forget about her strangeness, and her disturbing frown, and the long, thick, wiry hair growing out of that huge mole on her cheek.

Mrs Grimshaw's son is sitting beside his mother. He is much older than you and as usual he is reading a book. His left hand is twirling his fuzzy black hair and his right eyebrow twitches constantly, something you don't remember him doing last year. You wish he wasn't reading a book, because if he wasn't he'd probably be throwing stones as far as he could into the sea, or he'd be looking for flat stones to skim off the top of the water. Last summer he broke his own record and made a stone skim fourteen times. You were there to see it, though you weren't quick enough to count the fourteen skims. Peter was. Peter has brains to beat the band, your mother says. Your father says that he's a peculiar boy, though you are unsure what he means by this.

You walk across the stones, choosing each stone carefully to step on. You like the large round flat ones. Up near the prom, the stones are bigger and dry. The soles of your shoes make a small rasping sound as they scrape off them. As you get closer to the sea the stones form a little hill, and this can be tricky because they move beneath your feet. Near the water, the wet stones have a different colour. They are also much smaller. You have no idea why the stones are smaller near the sea and you don't remember ever noticing this before. You will ask Peter when he stops reading his book and twirling his hair and twitching his eyebrow.

Your mother is calling you. She is putting up her umbrella. You hadn't even noticed it was raining. You never mind the rain, because you'll be getting wet anyway when you go for a swim. She beckons to you to come. If your father was here there'd be no need to leave the beach because he always says a bit of rain won't kill anyone. You take a long time, dragging your feet along the stones as you go because you know your mother is going to go back to the house and there is nothing to do in the house except play with your cars and your soldiers and you can do that all day long in your real home.

By the time you get to the top of the beach you are already crying and it's only your first day.

'Poor Charlie', your mother says, pulling you to her and squeezing you, your arms hanging numbly at your sides like a puppet.

'Poor Charlie', repeats Peter, but you know by the sound of his voice that he isn't sorry for you at all, that if you turn your head to look at him he'll be smiling.

And you do. And he is.

Ten thousand is your new number. You like all the noughts. Yesterday, your second day down at the beach, you made a big 10,000 with lots of little stones that you'd carried up to the prom. You showed it to your mother and she seemed very happy.

'I didn't know you could count to 10,000', she said, and she smiled that smile of hers that is for you and you alone.

Peter arrives. He is in his swimming togs.

'Good boy, Peter', your mother says, 'I'm delighted you're here. I've to get a few messages in the town. Will you look after Charlie for a while? I won't be long'.

'I'll try and make sure he doesn't drown, Mrs Franklin'.

'You should never make jokes about a thing like that', your mother says crossly. 'You should never make jokes about drowning, Peter'.

Peter has gone red. Very red. You want to laugh, but are afraid to because your mother is so cross and when she's cross like this anything might happen. If you're not careful you could find yourself back in the house for the day while Peter is swimming and skimming stones. You don't want to miss a full day on the beach with Peter so you bite your lip and force back the laugh that very nearly burst out of you and onto the busy prom. Everything's all right, though, because your mother is now opening her purse and is taking out some coins and is giving them to Peter.

'Don't mind me, Peter', she says, 'I'm terrified of the water. Just be careful. Buy yourself and Charlie an ice-cream after your swim'.

And then she is gone, and it's just you and Peter here beside the stony beach and before you know it he's running across the stones and into the water, shouting, 'Last one in's a sissy!' You run across the stones after him and you charge into the water, forgetting that you still have your new khaki shorts on, and the orange and blue

striped t-shirt you got for your birthday. If your mother
sees you …

You stop halfway in, the water already up to your waist,
and you look up towards where you last saw your mother,
to check if she has seen you, but you're safe, there's no sign
of her, so you turn back to the sea and without a moment's
thought you dive into the water and swim out to Peter,
who is out of his depth already.

Tonight your mother and your father have the Grimshaws
in. That means you can stay up late. You were hoping that
Peter would come, too. He always used to come. When
you ask Mrs Grimshaw where Peter is, she says to your
mother, not to you, she ignores you completely even
though it was you who asked the question, 'Peter's at
home watching *The Virginian*. He never misses an episode'.
They leave you standing in the hall while they go into the
sitting room. Your mother comes back out after a short
time with the Grimshaws' overcoats which she hangs on
the hallstand.

'Mammy, can I go next door and watch *The Virginian*
with Peter?' you ask.

Your mother is looking forward to this night with the
Grimshaws. She's been baking half the day. There are
enough fairy cakes and chocolate crispies and lemon
meringues to last a week. And a Madeira cake. Your
mother must think the Grimshaws have never seen a cake,
which couldn't be true because Mrs Grimshaw is very fat.
She's actually the fattest person you've ever seen, that's if
you don't count Fatso, the boy in fifth class, who can't run
he's so fat. Your mother says that he has a big problem and
if someone doesn't do something his heart will give out.
'Why will his heart give out and not his huge tummy?' you
asked her once, and she laughed so hard you thought she
was going to burst. Your mother says the strangest things
sometimes. She's looking at you now and you know what

she's thinking: *If I let Charlie go next door, he'll be out of my hair and I can have a grand night.*

She's also thinking that it's a bit too late for you to be out of the house.

Once, you were sitting at the top of the stairs in your proper home and you heard your mother and your father talking about you and whether they would leave you in the school you were in, where you weren't at all happy, or put you in another school, which cost more money and was further away. You remember your mother saying, 'It's a dilemma, Pat. I don't know what the best thing to do is'. You know she's in another dilemma now and you wish you knew how to help her make the right decision. You want to say, 'Mammy, when you put me in my new school that was a good dilemma, and if you let me go next door to watch *The Virginian* with Peter that will be another good dilemma', but you know it won't come out right because whenever you try to talk like your parents you make a mess of it and all they do is laugh and make fun of you.

'Please', is what you end up saying, and that is all it takes because she doesn't even say, 'I'll ask your father', but instead wastes no time in putting on your coat and tying a scarf around your neck, even though it isn't cold, and she's opening the front door and kissing you and saying, 'I'll not let on to your father. He probably wouldn't mind, but you know how he is about Peter. Come back straight after *The Virginian* is over'.

And so here you are walking down the short path to the gate, lifting it as you open it so that it doesn't scrape along the ground, running along the footpath to the Grimshaw's gate, pushing it open and listening for the squeak, but the squeak from last year is gone. Mr Grimshaw must have poured oil on the hinge because there is no noise now as you push open the gate and close it behind you and walk up the short path to the front door.

And now you're standing on your toes to reach the door knocker and you manage to lift it and you let it fall onto the shiny brass and the sound is loud and strange and it hurts your ears.

Everything about the next day and the day after and the day after that is different to all the days that have ever gone before. Something terrible has happened; no, two terrible things have happened. In your heart you know the second one is the worst by far, because Peter isn't coming back, Peter will never be coming back. Everyone knows about Peter not coming back, and that makes it a little easier for you to deal with. The other thing, the thing that happened first, no one but you and Peter know about that, and now that Peter is dead you're the only one who knows. He warned you not to tell anyone, he even told you that no one would believe you if you did tell, and because you don't really know or understand what happened and because you don't know what words to use if you did try to tell someone, you are stuck in a place you were never in before and you don't like it there, but you don't know how to get out.

So you stay in the house with Aunt Margaret and Uncle John and they're trying hard to be nice to you, but you can see how shocked they are, they can't hide it, you think maybe they don't have words to describe how Peter died. But you do. You saw him hanging there, just like in *The Virginian*, when the angry mob ganged up on that poor Indian and put his head through the noose and spooked his horse so it galloped away, leaving him dangling in the air. You hated that part, and you tried to look away, but Peter grabbed you and made you look at it, which made you even more upset. That's when he pulled you to the floor.

Aunt Margaret and Uncle John decide to take you down to the seafront. You don't really want to go, but you don't want to upset them. You don't want to upset anyone anymore. So the three of you walk down the road in the sunshine and when you get to the prom you are amazed to see that the world hasn't stopped, that there are lots and lots of people having a good time while Peter is being lowered into the ground. Last December you watched Grandad's coffin being lowered into his grave. That's what happens to dead people, they get put in a big wooden box and they lower the box into a huge hole in the ground. That's where Peter is going today, into a huge hole in the ground. There's a small part of you that is glad, but the main part of you is very confused and sad.

Uncle John buys you an ice cream. It's a Bo-Peep. He buys one for Aunt Margaret, and he buys a Palm Grove choc ice for himself. You wonder why he didn't buy three choc ices. He knows you love Palm Grove choc ices. It doesn't seem fair that he got to eat a choc ice and you and Aunt Margaret only got a Bo-Peep. All of a sudden you begin to cry, and you feel stupid crying over something so silly, but you can't stop. You stand beside the kiosk under the hot August sun and there are crowds of people everywhere having a good time and all you can do is cry.

BULLY

A problem arose on Bill's first day. Steve, who had been working in the tunnels all afternoon, went to talk to Griff in the Portakabin as soon as the new man had left.

'What's the story with Bill?' Steve asked.

'How do you mean?'

'I mean how in the name of fuck did he get the job?'

'Only two candidates applied'.

'Did the other guy have no legs or something?'

'Actually, he was a she. Two spectacular legs but more at home on a catwalk than on a potato ridge. She looked like she couldn't turn a sod if her life depended on it'.

Steve's permanent frown deepened.

'Is there a problem with Bill?' Griff asked. 'He seems keen. He's a bit OTT, I'll grant you that, but Jesus, what a physique! The man is the size of Ben Bulben'.

'He's a big fucker sure enough', Steve said, and shuffled off to his car.

The bullying took place when no one else was around to witness or to overhear. Nervy by nature, Steve was now routinely tense and constantly on his guard. He was even wary going home, convinced that Bill had tailed him one evening, just to see where he lived. He had no idea why this was happening, why Bill had chosen him. It seemed random yet he guessed it wasn't.

Steve reported the bullying to Griff. Bill denied everything. He was so convincing that Griff began to wonder if Steve was losing the plot. Then Steve made a formal complaint and everything changed, their long-standing working relationship becoming charged with an awkward tension. Steve presented his complaint to Griff in neat handwriting, four long foolscap pages, detailing every single incident since the alleged bullying began. He impressed upon Griff the need for caution and discretion. Bill, he warned, was not to be told until the committee had discussed the matter.

'Has he made a formal complaint?' Bill asked Griff the following day.

They were in the tiny office, Bill and Griff. It was lunchtime. The others were in the canteen.

'I'm not at liberty to say', Griff fumbled. Later, when it was all over, he couldn't remember the circumstances surrounding the disclosure to Bill. Had it been deliberate? Or had Bill, in his sly and manipulative way, managed to prise it out of him? Whatever the explanation, it had been an unforgivable act of disloyalty towards someone he had worked with for eight years.

'You do know you're obliged by law to notify the accused once a formal complaint has been made?' Bill said.

'I didn't know that'.

'And that the accused has the right to read the complaint once it has been lodged?'

'I didn't know that, either'.

'May I?' said Bill, holding out a hand as bulky as a boxing glove.

He read it slowly, making a mental note of every incident Steve had described so precisely. It was all there, a true and accurate account. He handed back the four pages, shaking his head ruefully as he did so.

'I don't know what to say, Griff. There is nothing there that I recognise. I honestly don't know what's going on in that man's mind. He's not well'.

'Are you saying he made it all up?'

'That's exactly what I'm saying. There isn't a word of truth in there. He's basically accusing me of carrying out a campaign of intimidation against him. Why would I do that? How would I do that? Where would I even find the time to do that? He may not be on my guest list, but that doesn't mean I'm going to threaten to beat him up. It's clear he has a problem, and that he's chosen me to dump his issues on. I'll be lodging my own counter complaint. I'm not letting the fucker get away with soiling my good name'.

He had let his anger out of its cage, just for a moment, and he brought it under control quickly.

'Thanks for being so supportive and understanding', he said now to Griff. 'You've been put in a difficult situation. It's not my intention to make trouble. That's not my style. But you have to understand I can't let Steve get away with this. If he continues with these allegations, it will end up badly for everyone. I'm a nice guy with a big heart, but I'm not a man you'd want to cross. I won't roll over for anyone, especially if some deranged idiot is making false and damaging allegations against me'.

The issue went to the committee. Every member had an opinion, and no one opinion was the same. Disagreements broke out. None of them had any experience of dealing with bullying in the workplace.

Meanwhile, the bullying intensified. Though less frequent, it became more malicious and intimidating. Steve lost weight, and didn't always come to work. Bill went out of his way to be helpful to everyone, and not just at work. He gave a dig out to an influential committee member, spending two afternoons on the member's estate helping to plant several hundred trees. He dealt with the constant gossip at work about the 'Steve/Bill situation' like a practiced diplomat.

'I've promised the committee not to discuss the matter with anyone. I'm sorry it has come to this. I'm completely at sea as to why this is happening'.

The co-workers were divided. Most wanted to believe Steve, yet accepting his accusations as truth put them in an impossible situation with Bill, who came across as nothing more than a big, harmless oaf who had an unfortunate knack of rubbing people up the wrong way. There were others who had never got on with Steve and who were happy to accept Bill's side of the story. Mostly, though, it was a period of great unease and tension, multiplied a hundred fold anytime Steve and Bill were in the canteen at the same time. On those occasions, no one knew which way to look.

What couldn't be ignored was the shocking decline in Steve's wellbeing, both physical and psychological. Bill, on the other hand, appeared to be thriving. He ate heartily, he continued to tell his terrible, frequently offensive jokes – and loudly. As Steve appeared to diminish before their eyes, everything with Bill became increasingly loud and large. He filled any space he was in.

Yet he was also a master of the understatement, the whispered threat, the stealthy movement behind a tunnel or a line of fruit bushes, wherever Steve was working. Steve was convinced it was only a matter of time before the verbal threats became physical. There had been one incident, near the beginning, when Steve, no weakling, confronted Bill, in fury at Bill's persistent needling. Bill's right hand came up quickly and grabbed Steve's fist and held it, vice-like. He stared down at Steve and twisted his wrist slowly, letting him know that if he wanted to he could snap it. Steve didn't know anyone who had a grip like it. It was as if Bill was in possession of a lethal weapon, and worse, was eager to use it.

The issue divided the committee, just as it had divided the workers. Griff was caught in the middle and was no help to anyone. He tried his best, as was his way, but his best was dismal. He was out of his depth, had no training in these complex and emotionally-charged matters and worse, he was a poor judge of character. He couldn't see what was blindingly obvious: that a man had entered their well-balanced and amiable group and was causing havoc, not just to a single, singled-out member of their tiny community, but now to the entire organisation.

The committee discussed little else during these times. It met often. A sub-committee, hurriedly established, interviewed, first Steve, then Bill. Steve came across as a victim, but not one you would warm to. His language was enflamed, his tone accusatory. He said he was dismayed that the members of the committee, even his boss, refused to see the obvious. He was unpleasantly – some thought *unnecessarily* – angry. He accused the committee of negligence and incompetence. He didn't win over many friends.

Bill, in contrast, was contrite – 'I'm sorry, I seem to be the source of all this turmoil'. He was calm, expressed puzzlement. He was affable, helpful. He offered a hand of friendship to Steve – in Steve's absence, naturally enough. He said he felt sorry for Steve and offered to do anything the committee asked to solve the awkward situation.

The matter came to an unexpected and abrupt end when Steve, his nerves shot as a result of the relentless bullying, and his will worn down by the lack of support around him and the whispered conversations he knew were taking place behind his back, applied for and was granted extended sick leave. He didn't know it at the time, but he would never again set foot inside the gates of the place that for almost a decade had been a second home and a safe haven from all the shit that he had left behind in Cork.

Less than a week after Steve took his leave, Bill, uncontrollable addict that he was, began the whole thing over again, with a different member of staff. As soon as the committee learned of this new allegation, they summoned him and fired him. Bill accused them of prejudice, incompetence, of breaking the law. He left, claiming he would sue. He was never heard of again.

The committee went back to doing what it did best, holding monthly meetings, talking in ever-expanding circles, planning the Christmas party, but otherwise putting off making decisions until the next meeting.

The workers, relieved that the long-running and troublesome affair was resolved, resumed normal operations, though the subject and the endless discussions around it never did go away.

Griff went on holidays to try to erase the entire episode, but he was unable to get his last encounter with Steve out of his mind. He had held out his hand in the car park, in a gesture of friendship and goodwill. Steve gazed at the outstretched hand for several seconds, as if bewildered by the gesture, then raised his eyes and stared at Griff.

'I'd always thought of you as a friend, but honestly, I'd be inclined to shake Bill's hand quicker than I'd shake yours'.

Then he got into his car and drove away.

Making Sandwiches

'I wouldn't let him make me a sandwich', Andrea said.

'Brian? You must be kidding'.

'It's not *just* his grubby little fat fingers. It's his whole wardrobe. All his clothes look like they were rejected by Oxfam'.

'That's so cruel', he said, smiling.

'Can you imagine the state of his flat?' she asked.

'I'd rather not'.

'A pigsty would be plush in comparison', she said.

Brian rejoined them at their table in the empty lounge bar of the Seaview Hotel.

'What's so funny?' he asked, guardedly. Andrea had noticed that he was always more uptight whenever Damien was around.

'This place', said Andrea. 'It's hilarious. It's like being in a time warp'.

'There's always the Anchor or Gogarty's'.

'They're just pubs, Brian. This place is a parallel world. Anyway, what were we talking about?'

Damien looked into the middle distance and furrowed his brow. 'It wouldn't have been EcoCeltic, by any chance?'

EcoCeltic, the environmental lobby group of which Andrea and Brian were members, seemed to be all they ever talked about.

'Smart arse', said Andrea.

Brian gave her a furtive look. He started to say something, then stopped and began to chew his lower lip.

'What is it, Brian? Come on, out with it. It'll be a gem, I know it'. Andrea's sarcasm knew no bounds.

Brian took a deep breath and went for it.

'If we can put pressure on the local counsellors, I mean real pressure that they can't ignore ...'

'Yehhh', groaned Andrea.

'They'll then put pressure on their TDs, and if we can get enough momentum behind the campaign, the Minister may have to do a U-turn'.

His face seemed worn out by the earnestness he forced it to wear day in and day out.

'That's simplistic stuff, Brian', Andrea said, turning serious. 'The counsellors don't give a shit about us. Do you know what comes into their minds whenever EcoCeltic is mentioned? A bunch of nutters, that's what. You were there, Brian, don't give me that blank I-don't-know-what-you're-talking-about look. You were up to your knees in sea water trying to salvage the files, even as Elsa and what's-her-face ...'

'Heike', Brian prompted.

'... even as Elsa and Heike were throwing them over the harbour wall'.

Whenever Andrea shone her alarmingly caustic spotlight on Brian, which she did with a cruel frequency, his reaction was invariably the same – head lowered, eyes fastened on a point between his two worse-for-wear Docs.

'Poor Brian, did you have to get your teeny weeny feet wet?'

'That was four years ago', he said, still looking at the floor. 'Not that many people actually witnessed it', he added.

'It's lodged in their tiny brains, Brian. When they think of us and our office, that's what they see – a group of environmental nutters who couldn't organise a piss-up in Temple Bar. Going the political route is all well and good, and we'll do all that bullshit you suggest, lobbying those morons and trying to be persuasive and not calling them assholes, which is what they are. But that's not what's going to make the difference'.

Brian was too much in awe of Andrea, and too gormless, to feel admonished by her remarks. She could say anything to him and he would still think that she could do or say no wrong.

'What do *you* suggest?' he asked.

'Good old-fashioned people power. Street protests. A blockade of the harbour. A massive march to Dublin. There's any number of things we can do. We need to get the issue on national news'.

'A new golf course and forty-five holiday homes on the Atlantic seaboard is hardly national news material', Damien said.

'We'll make it national news material', Andrea said, her voice rising. 'How does a local issue make national news? By *making* it national news!'

'Right', said Damien. 'Whatever'. He stood up. 'Another Smithwicks, Brian?'

'Yeh, thanks, Daim'.

'Andrea?'

'Jesus, Damien, we're in the middle of an important discussion and all you can think about is another drink'.

'Well, do you want one or not?'

'Oh, go on then'.

The campaign office that the directors of EcoCeltic had appointed Andrea to re-establish and run for a trial period of a year was a small room on the third floor of a house on the main street. In it were crammed two filing cabinets, three small desks, two computers, a photocopier and Andrea. The other desks were at different times occupied by local EcoCeltic members who, apart from Brian who came in from two till five every weekday, seemed to come and go as the fancy or the guilt took them. Files and documents and press cuttings cluttered every available space, including the floor. It was a scene of utter chaos and one in which Andrea appeared to thrive. She called head office every day without fail, giving whoever was there to take the call an update on what was happening.

'We need a huge crowd', she enthused to Gráinne, a Tuesday volunteer up in Dublin who didn't know anything about Andrea's campaign. 'We need to show those bastard speculators that their money is useless against the power of the ordinary man or woman on the street. This demo is going to be the biggest ever seen in the south west'.

'I'm a bit worried', Damien said.

It was the weekend before the big event and he had come down from Dublin, ostensibly to see Andrea and to provide moral support, but really to suss out how the preparations were going. Andrea's increasingly excitable phone calls to him had set off alarm bells. He was fearful that her expectations had gone through the roof and he knew from past experience that nothing good could come from that. There was no questioning her drive and her passion, but it was hard to ignore the fact that she was a divisive force when cooperation and goodwill were needed instead. He had to see the situation at first hand.

After a day going around the town, talking to some of the volunteers and a few dozen locals, his worst fears were confirmed.

'What's worrying you, sweetie?' she asked him, teasingly, hanging on to his arm, as they set out on a walk by the sea in the late evening. She was on a quiet high, borne out of the excitement of the campaign and by the presence of Damien at her side.

'I don't think you're going to get the response from the townspeople that you seem to be expecting'.

'Don't be silly', she said. 'Anyway, what do you know about the townspeople? You don't even live here'.

'I live in the real world, Andrea'.

'Are you saying that I don't?'

'You're too trusting of people. You think that when someone says they'll turn up on the day, they actually will. They might mean it at the time, but most of them will be found wanting when you need them most. That's the way people are. Especially in small town Ireland. People don't like to say no to your face'.

'You've got it all wrong', she said. 'The people around here are one-hundred-per-cent against this development'.

'Not from what I've heard'.

'You've just arrived. How would you know anything about what the people are thinking?'

'You know me, I find it easy talking to people and a lot of those I've spoken to feel uneasy about the campaign. There's a view, and it's pretty widespread from what I can gather, that the development will be good for the town'.

'I can't believe you're saying this. Of all people. Even Brian ...'

'Brian! What the fuck has Brian got to do with anything?'

'At least Brian is supportive'.

'That's because he fancies you'.

She glared at him. 'I didn't think you did pathetic', she said.

They walked a while in silence, her arm no longer entwined in his. A light breeze cooled the warm afternoon air. She was wearing a black skirt and a flecked grey sleeveless blouse. Her arms were tanned a light, silky brown and the outer strands of her soft, black hair moved in the breeze.

'I'm sorry', he said. 'Brian's probably right. He's from here, he should know'.

'Brian's an asshole', she said, tearfully, 'and he's totally irrelevant. But you, I rely on you and your support. I can't believe you've been going behind my back'.

'I haven't been going behind your back. I'm trying to protect you'.

'You could have fooled me'.

Thursday arrived and with it came heavy and prolonged rain. Damien's abiding memory, when he would dwell on it later, was of a sodden Andrea standing on her own at the entrance to the harbour, a barely-legible placard in her hands, the rain sweeping up the bay and lashing her back. Defiant till the end. He and Brian could see her from where they sat, at the window of the Anchor. Damien had tried his best to persuade her to come inside, to accept that the weather had got the better of them.

Only a handful of supporters had turned up in the morning. By eleven they were soaked through. Some left then, telling Andrea that they were going home to change into dry clothes. The rest left after midday, and offered a variety of excuses. No one returned. The media hadn't shown at midday for the promised photo call. Not even the local paper. By lunchtime, only Andrea, Damien and Brian were left. At two, Brian announced that he'd had enough. Andrea accused him of being a traitor to the cause. Damien watched him go in to the Anchor, then turned to Andrea and was about to try to persuade her to call it a day when he caught a look in her eye that forced his words back down his throat. If you leave me here on my own, the look said, you leave me forever.

At five o'clock he did leave her. He had remained beside her the entire, ridiculous, farcical day. He had supported her through the torrents of rain, to the point when their placards had become soggy and stupid looking, and they themselves were so wet and miserable that Damien could practically hear what the people slowing down in their cars to have a gawk were saying.

'We must look completely idiotic', he said, finally. 'No one could possibly take us seriously, looking like we do. Not only are we going to catch pneumonia, we're going to surpass the myth that Elsa and Heike have become. We'll forever be remembered as the crazy nutters who stayed out all day on the wettest day of the year and got nowhere'.

'We *have* got somewhere', she said defiantly.

'No we haven't. If anything, by staying out here all day, just the two of us, we've highlighted the fact that there *is* no local support for the campaign'.

The coldness of her stare made him uneasy, yet he had made up his mind.

'I never would have thought you'd turn out to be such a sad loser', she said.

He had to return to Dublin the next day. He tried to persuade her to come with him, but she wasn't talking to him and he was left with no option but to leave her there and hope that her anger would dissolve over the coming days.

He called her from his flat that night, but there was no answer. He rang every evening, and when the weekend finally came around he got on a bus and made the journey back down, only to have his worst fears confirmed. She'd moved out.

He found Brian moping in the Anchor, a pint of Smithwicks in front of him.

'Did she tell you where she was going?' he asked him.

'Nope'.

'Did you ask?'

'Nope'.

'What the fuck is wrong with you?'

But Brian couldn't reply, couldn't even manage another 'nope'. Damien stood over him and watched as he broke down crying.

'For fuck's sake, Brian, anyone would think it was you she was going out with. Get a grip'.

He left him there and walked the few hundred metres to the Seaview Hotel. There was an American couple sitting where he and Andrea always sat. It was the only curved seat in the lounge, and it had a stunning view across the bay. At a certain time of the day, the sun's angle would send a shaft of sunlight through the bay window, directly onto the circular pine table. Unlike the disastrous weather that descended on the town on the day of the protest, today was all blue sky and warm sunshine. He took a seat at the bar and ordered a pint and waited for the American couple to finish their drinks. When they had left, he would cross the room and take his place beside where Andrea had always insisted on sitting, declaring that the view was better from that exact spot. He would sit there on the faded green fabric and he would drink as many pints as it took for the sun to move across the sky. He calculated that there were at least five hours to go before the intimate light show would commence, the departing sun shining its much too late light onto the faded varnish, before moving off the table and sidling off along the threadbare carpet. Andrea once said it reminded her of a golden snake sliding in slow motion across the floor. Damien always felt the shaft's departure was like a curtain closing slowly at the end of the play.

The American couple ordered more drinks, which meant that his plan would have to be put on hold, until, that is, they got hungry enough to head off to the dining room. He ordered a second pint. The bar was fine, he liked sitting on his own at bars. He didn't always have plans, but he knew he was at his best when he had one; or rather, he was at his most vulnerable when he had none. Five hours was nothing when your life had taken a bad turn. There was no place he would rather be than sprawled out on that curved seat over there, waiting for the sun to pass the time.

BEGIN WITH LONELINESS

The plaque on the door read, *Henry Thompson, psychotherapist, specialising in issues relating to loneliness.*

I buzzed the intercom and a man's voice, soft and tentative, as if he was wary of projecting his voice into the busy street, into the open, treacherous air, said, 'Henry Thompson's clinic. How may I help you?'

I placed my lips to the intercom. 'My name is Ellen Nash. I'm enquiring about the consultations'.

'On loneliness or unhappiness?'

'You give consultations on unhappiness?'

'Actually, we deal with three core issues at the clinic. Loneliness. Unhappiness. And what I like to call General Lethargy of the Spirit'.

I was processing this information when the intercom buzzed and the lock on the door clicked.

Henry Thompson was waiting for me at the top of the stairs. Really I knew nothing about him, other than what Gina had told me, which was, typical of Gina, deliberately misleading and vague. The house seemed unusually quiet for a clinic. As if reading my mind, he said, as he indicated an open door on the landing for me to go through, 'I'm on my own today. The others are at a funeral. I drew the short straw'.

We stood in a square room soaked in a sombre light that hovered above a sullen grey carpet. It was not a cheerful room. Again, as if he had a direct view into my thoughts, he said, 'I like to leave the light off. Atmospherics are all important in this line of work'.

I had never thought about the importance or otherwise of atmospherics in a shrink's consultation rooms, but now that Henry Thompson had mentioned it, I found myself agreeing with the sentiment. It made perfect sense, having the right atmospherics in situations that by their very nature are tense and potentially volatile.

'So tell me', he said, settling into an old, worn-out armchair, 'what prompted you to ring the intercom?'

I looked around for a chair. There was none.

'Is this the consultation?'

'It's the prelim. We conduct the prelim in here. Is there something wrong?'

At other, more confident times in my life, when my tolerance for people who didn't fit into my carefully-controlled world was at basement level, I might have turned and walked back down the stairs, but things hadn't been going well of late, and in any case, despite the strangeness of the set-up, I had a sense of purpose for the first time in a while. I was also in dire need of something to latch on to, and Henry Thompson's consultation rooms were as good a place as any to find that hook that continued to elude me.

'Nothing's wrong. I saw the plaque, and I rang'.

'You're lonely?'

'Yes'.

'Unhappy?'

'Uh-huh'.

'Low spirits?'

'Pretty low'.

'The consultations are not cheap'.

I looked around the room. At the large window that looked out on the backs of houses. At the grey filing cabinet in the corner. At the single, crooked shelf on one of the walls on which were stacked a half dozen books, the titles of which I couldn't read from where I stood.

'How many will I need to do?'

'That depends on the progress we make. The consultations can be ongoing, or there might be a breakthrough early on. It's really impossible to tell'.

What I said next I didn't mean to say, but sometimes that's how I am, saying or doing things on an impulse. The fact that I said it at all suggested an unlikely ease of mind, which in itself was as unexpected as Gina walking down the landing and entering the room we were in. I felt a smile form on my lips, for I was beginning to feel at home here in this bare and beautiful house.

'You're on your own here, aren't you?'

'Today I am. As I said, the others are at a funeral'.

I didn't believe him. I felt certain that he was a one-man show up here in this languid atmosphere, in these hollow-sounding rooms. He probably expected me to leave then, but I had made up my mind to stay.

'Ok, let's do it'.

'Come again?'

'I want to book a consultation'.

'That's a positive step. When are you thinking of?'

'Are you free right now?'

'I am, as it happens. It's one of those quiet days. Would you like to start with loneliness?'

'Either that or unhappiness'.

'Most people begin with loneliness. It seems to be a favoured starting point'.

'Loneliness it is, so'.

He rose from his armchair and left the room. 'Come this way', he called out from the landing.

I followed him down the corridor towards a room at the front of the house.

'Fate plays a part, of course'.

He was sitting behind a large mahogany desk, leaning forward in his chair, his elbows on the dark, lacquered wood, the backs of his entwined fingers propping up his bony chin. I stood at the threshold of the door, looking in. Apart from Henry Thompson, the chair he was sitting on, the large mahogany desk, and a folded wooden chair leaning against the blank wall opposite the two large windows that overlooked the street, the room was empty. The walls were bare. Not a shelf or a book in sight. A small, framed photo stood on the desk, its back to me. I walked across the room, picked up the chair, brought it to the desk, unfolded it and sat down.

'Fate sent you off this morning on your wanderings. Fate turned your eyes to the plaque on the door. Fate arranged that I would be here and that I would have a free appointment'.

'Has the session begun?'

'Sessions don't begin, they evolve. One moment we are conversing, the next we are in session. It is a mysterious process. Have you done anything like this before now?'

I took a deep breath before answering. My throat was dry and I looked around for a glass, for water, then remembered how devoid of objects the room was.

'I was seeing a psychiatrist for six years; off and on; more off than on if I'm being honest. Especially of late. We were rehashing old stuff and we were getting nowhere'.

'I see'.

A long, awkward silence ensued, its provenance unclear to me. As it stretched and as it gradually released its tension and eased into I guess a kind of manageability, we passed the time in looking out separate windows. He had positioned the desk near the window for this precise purpose, I suspected, for those difficult moments that could transmute into walls of silence or some kind of breakthrough. On the street below we looked at the same scene, yet I was sure he did not see what I saw. The thought broke through my silence.

'What do you see down below?' I asked.

'A lot of lonely people. A lot of unhappiness. A lot of lethargy'.

I could feel him looking at me.

'And you?' he asked. 'What do you see?'

'I see the ghost of Gina Traynor walking along the far pavement'.

'Which one is she?'

'She's wearing a purple hat'.

'I don't see anyone with a purple hat. When and how did she die?'

'She died five days ago. An overdose'.

I turned away from the window. Elusive when she was alive, now that Gina was dead she was everywhere.

'I'm tired of talking about myself', I said. 'And I don't want to talk about Gina. Let's talk about you'.

'There isn't much to talk about. In any case, it's your session'.

'Exactly'. I felt an irrepressible urge to take over. 'So tell me'.

I made him change places and I began the session. He proved to be a pliant, if morose, client. He wasn't verbose, yet what he said was to the point. He didn't waste words.

'After a while, people drift away', he said.

'Why do they drift away?' I prodded.

'Wouldn't you?'

This time it was me who began the long, awkward silence. We looked out our respective windows, though now I was looking through his, and he gazed through mine.

'What do you see now?' he asked.

'It's strange, but I see what you saw earlier. Lonely and unhappy people. Lethargy weighing everyone down'.

I was afraid to ask him what he saw, but he told me anyway.

'I see Gina. There, at the bus stop, on Waterloo Road. Do you see her?'

I looked, but I could see no one standing at the bus stop. I said as much. This seemed to please him. A hint of a smile stretched his thin lips as he continued to stare in the direction of the bus stop.

'Poor Gina', he said, after another long silence.

The light of the day was fading now, an observation I made vaguely, unimportantly. After all, I had had no plans for this day, so what did it matter that the hours were passing here in this large empty room?

'Why do you put yourself through all this?' I asked.

'How do you mean?'

'You sit in this empty house on your own every day, listening to strangers telling you about their various shades and stages of loneliness and unhappiness, you enquire into the health of their lethargic spirit …'

I trailed off. He was clearly an unhappy man. What right did I have to twist the knife?

'And your point is?' he said, turning from the window to look me in the eye.

'Let's go back to where we were', I said, rising from his chair.

'No. Stay. It's good that you are there. It feels right'.

Actually, it did. It had been a while since I'd felt like this. Like I was in the right place at the right time.

'Finish what you were going to say', he said.

'I just wanted to know why a lonely, unhappy, spiritually-lethargic man would want to listen to other lonely, unhappy, spiritually-lethargic people all day long'.

There it was, that bluntness of mine, that had ruined so many friendships and had sent several lovers packing.

'Is Gina still at the bus stop?' I asked, mainly to remove his gaze from me, but also because a part of my consciousness had held on to the image of Gina ever since I'd seen her with her purple hat a couple of hours earlier, or was it a couple of minutes ago? Time had taken on an unidentifiable quality here in Henry Thompson's consultation rooms.

'Do you want to tell me about Gina?' he asked.

'I'd rather we talked about you'.

He began to talk about the loneliness that had kept him company all through his life. How it had never been a crutch, more like a reliable friend.

'Does your unhappiness stem from your loneliness?' I enquired.

'They feed off each other'.

'Snap', I said softly, as much to myself as to him.

'To tell the truth', he said very quietly, so quietly in fact that I had to lean towards him to catch the words, 'I've been pretty miserable for as long as I can remember'.

Our unhappiness session took us into the early part of the night. The sounds coming up from the street had changed. There were more cars, commuters returning home from work. It had begun to drizzle, and the noise of the wet tyres was a long, continuous, sibilant whish. Neither of us suggested turning on a light. The room, dark now, was invaded by shadows and twinkles and sudden, startling flashes from the headlights of cars swinging left at the corner of Waterloo Road. Occasionally, I thought of Gina Traynor, and how her loneliness and her unhappiness had acted like a magnet for me in school, how it had kept my own depression company. And not just in school. Later, too. It was really hard for me to think about Gina.

The longest silence of the day was now becoming warm and familiar. Since I was a teenager, I had experienced acute paranoia over long silences in company, yet here we were, Henry Thompson and me, soaking it up, breathing it in, being replenished by it. As the cars began to dwindle in number, I said a quiet prayer that neither of us would break the lush, sensual silence. We looked out of our respective windows, and sometimes we looked at each other. We were each, I think, not a little bemused that the other was still there. As the clock on the corner of the street struck ten, Henry spoke.

'I suppose we could leave lethargy of the spirit for another session. What do you think?'

'Definitely. I wouldn't be able to rise to lethargy at this stage in the day'.

'Do you need to use the bathroom before you go?'

'No harm'.

'It's down in the basement. The door at the end of the corridor. It has a sign on it. I'll sit here in the dark a while longer'.

The street lamps cast a pale yellow light into the house, sufficient to guide me down the stairs to the basement. It was too dark to see at the bottom, so I switched on a light. Two doors on the left led off the narrow corridor. The bathroom door was at the end. I opened the first door and switched on the main light.

Gina's purple hat was lying on the single bed. So this was where she had slept. My eyes were drawn to a framed photo on her bedside locker. It was identical to the one on Henry's mahogany desk, and when I picked it up I wasn't surprised to see that the photo in the small frame was the same. Gina and Ellen sitting at a café, a glass of red wine in front of each, both girls – for that is what we were – smiling at the camera.

I placed the photo back on the locker and, without thinking about what I was doing, I picked up Gina's hat and put it on at an angle, the way she had always worn it. I switched off the light and closed the door behind me and opened a door into a small kitchen. The light from the corridor threw a dull spotlight on a round table in the corner with two wooden chairs. Although I wanted to see Gina sitting in one of the chairs, I knew she was no longer here but stranded out there somewhere, waiting at imaginary bus stops, wandering along imaginary streets.

In the bathroom I stole a look at myself in the mirror. I was like a different person with Gina's purple hat on my head. Part Gina, part Ellen. I sensed we were one and the same person. I liked the feeling of being two people, especially when one of them was Gina.

I heard Henry's footsteps descending the stairs. He was singing, very softly, a song Gina loved and which I'd been singing without realising it, possibly since putting on Gina's hat. Perhaps he had heard me, but I like to think he hadn't, that he'd started singing of his own accord. I opened the door of the bathroom and stood in the threshold, looking down the corridor. I think I may have been smiling, because I was filled with an incredibly warm feeling at that moment. I felt that Gina was present. Part of me knew she couldn't be, yet a deeper part was open to the possibility. When Henry appeared at the end of the corridor he stared at me and his mouth opened as if he was about to say something but no words came out.

'Henry', we said, and we walked towards him.

A Woman Like That

Sandy Keegan is used to getting her own way. She has won court cases against developers and has single-handedly stopped two developments from going ahead on the outskirts of the village. As a result, she has successfully divided the close-knit community into two distinct groups – those who think that she has brought only benefits to the community and those who think she's a royal pain in the ass who will get her comeuppance sooner rather than later.

During the short walk from her cottage to the shop this morning she has, for the second time this week, been forced to lean in to the roadside hedge in order to avoid being run over, this time by a truck carrying construction rubble.

'Pedestrians and cyclists have been driven off the roads', she complains to Kathleen, who owns the shop. 'It would make you sick in the stomach to listen to those useless fools in the government banging on about obesity and the need for regular exercise when in truth they don't give a damn if we're all run over'.

Kathleen, normally gregarious, is subdued in Sandy's presence. Still, she hasn't said a word for five minutes and decides she'd better say something so as not to seem rude.

'Would you not say it's the drivers themselves who are to blame?'

'Oh, honestly', Sandy says, causing Kathleen to immediately regret her intervention. 'It's the government that decides the road-building programme. The same government that regards pedestrians as third-class citizens. Just the other day I was almost run over by Freddy Fallon in his big black SUV. Isn't he part of the government you think is so great?'

She takes the cigarettes she has paid for and puts them in the pocket of her grey linen jacket and leaves the shop and walks to the bridge. The river moves lazily beneath her. She leans on the wall and looks down at the water and feels the morning sun warm the back of her bare neck. She lights a cigarette and draws on it and looks up the river in the direction of Teddy's hut. She knows what she is going to say, but she has not been able to get a handle on what he might say in reply. Teddy is a tricky piece of work and she will not underestimate him. He gives the impression of idleness, both of the body and the brain, and of a lazy kind of stupidity, yet no one who knows him, and especially those who have had dealings with him, regard him as anything other than the shrewdest of operators who, when set on a course, will use any means at his disposal to get his own way.

Sandy knows this about him. A year ago, he objected to a holiday home development along the river. On her way to the shop this morning she remembered the doggedness with which he pursued his objective. He has me to thank for overturning that decision, she reflected, as she rounded the last bend and the shop came into view. Teddy's bicycle was leaning against the side wall of the shop. Moments later Teddy himself emerged. He was carrying a plastic bag which Sandy knew would contain his provisions for the day; the *Irish Independent*, a sliced pan, a carton of milk, a few slices of ham and a couple of tomatoes, perhaps a packet of cheddar, if he'd none left up above. A pound of unsalted butter if he'd run out. He mounted the bicycle and cycled through the open gate beside the bridge and disappeared. In a few minutes, she thought, he will be in his default position, sitting on his arse on the wooden chair, the kettle on the boil, the bread in the toaster, the transistor tuned to Radio One. Settled for the day, bar the interruptions by the cruisers and barges passing through the lock, and which he has to see to. The middle of July is a busy time on the river, but Teddy will make sure the boaters themselves will do most of the heavy work. If it's a boat with an elderly couple, or one full of women of a certain age, he will see them right. The others can look after themselves, with a minimum of overseeing on his part.

Sandy goes over in her mind one last time her carefully crafted speech. She is looking forward to the fencing match, for as tricky and obstinate as he is, she believes he is no match for her. Her English teacher once told her that she had a remarkable brain and no manners. Sandy has always been of the view that the assessment was overly harsh, yet she has never denied the fundamental truth of it. All her life she has said what is on her mind and has never much cared who she might offend in the process.

The postman pulls up beside her in his green van, leans across the passenger seat and calls to her through the open window.

'I've some post here for you. Will I leave it up at the house?'

She knows the postman well. During the protracted series of objections and appeals to the riverside development last year he was a regular caller, bearing registered letters and documents and a steady stream of hate mail. She leans in the window and looks through the envelopes he has left on the seat for her.

'Nothing that can't wait', she says, withdrawing her head. 'Drop them in my letterbox, if you don't mind'.

'I saw you gazing lovingly in Teddy's direction. Are you and he still at loggerheads?'

'We were never at loggerheads. We just don't see eye to eye. He has his way of doing things and I have mine'.

The Waterways people have been doing some improvement work along the old towpath. Sandy is of the opinion that the work was unnecessary and carried out by imbeciles. She's been in touch with the Waterways office and with the local representatives, including Freddie Fallon. Too many trees cut down, she told them, heavy-handed work carried out by people who don't know a tree from a boulder. She steps gingerly along the unfinished path, which is now an uneven, potholed, muddy road. Once she nearly goes over on her weak ankle, which sets her fuming once more, and it is in this frame of mind that she approaches Teddy's hut. But when she gets to the large window and looks inside, the hut is empty. She pushes open the door and is greeted by the smell of freshly-toasted bread and by the sound of the electric kettle coming to boiling point.

'Looking for anyone in particular?'

His lightness of foot catches her off guard, coming up behind her like that. And after all this time knowing him, his bulky, six-foot-four frame still manages to unsettle her. She is flustered, and doesn't know why.

'You're looking prettier by the day, Sandy. To what do I owe the honour?'

And now he has done what she didn't think him capable of – he has attempted charm, and on her of all people. Worse, he has carried it off with an ease that throws her.

'You probably know why I'm here', she says, looking up to where his face looks down at her from a frame of blue sky.

The bright glare of the morning light dazzles her, so that she blinks repeatedly. Also – and she doesn't know why this should be – her mouth is dry and the words snag in her throat. She brushes down her skirt, even though it doesn't need attention.

'I'd have a fair idea', he says.

He is smiling, but there is a hardness, even a cruelty, in his eyes. Once again, he has made her feel uncomfortable. She has never seen him wear that expression before and with a jolt realizes it is the look of a man who knows he has the upper hand, who believes he has won the battle before it can even commence.

'Why, Teddy?'

'Why, Teddy what?'

'Why did you sell to those people?'

'I'm not sure that's any of your business'.

'You know I'll object. I can't not object'.

Her voice has an edge to it that she scarcely recognises. She is on the back foot and she knows she must gain the upper hand quickly or Teddy will make a fool of her. She cannot believe that she has allowed this to happen.

'I'd be very disappointed if you didn't', he says.

The smile is still there, but the hardness has left the eyes. Sandy launches into her prepared speech, but to her dismay the words do not flow easily. She ends up making a disjointed statement, and she gets personal, something she was determined to avoid, knowing how counterproductive it would be.

'Part of me thinks you've lost the plot entirely, Teddy, and part of me thinks greed has got the better of you. You do know this will make you even more unpopular than you already are, though I suppose that is unlikely to give you any cause for concern'.

The hardness in Teddy's eyes has returned. They are alert and intense and their directness unflinching.

'For God's sake, Teddy, for the sake of the village and everyone in it will you drop this nonsense of yours?' she blurts out in a voice she barely recognizes as her own.

She looks around the empty hut in an aimless gesture, then catches herself doing something with her hair, and stops. She brushes down her skirt again.

'It's a done deal, Sandy. No going back'.

'I will do everything in my power to stop it. You'll be sorry you went against me'.

He has slipped by her and he has put four teabags into the pot and is now pouring the boiled water on top of the bags.

'You did a fine job on the holiday homes objection, sure enough', he says. 'If it hadn't been for your persistence, Sandy, and your ability to tie everyone in knots with your verbal dexterity, we'd both be looking at a construction site from where we're standing'.

'I've never understood why you set yourself against almost everyone else in the parish', she says.

She is still standing at the doorway, but now that Teddy has moved away from her she feels suddenly emboldened.

'What did it matter to you whether they built a hundred holiday homes or not?'

Teddy's instinct is to remain silent. Sometimes words, even carefully chosen ones, can get a man into a lot of trouble. He isn't entirely sure what lies at the source of the charged atmosphere that has invaded his quiet little hut, or what has brought on the embarrassing display of pent-up emotion from the normally controlled Sandy Keegan. Of course, he has his suspicions. It is not, he realizes, entirely unexpected; indeed, he has had an idea for some time now of her feelings towards him. What interests him more than anything is his suspicion that she herself has not seen it coming, that she is only now, this moment, becoming aware of her feelings. It is like watching an accident in slow motion – he knows he shouldn't look, knows he has no right to even act out the role play, but he finds himself incapable of withdrawing. The tension she has created intrigues him and he feels compelled to see the drama through to whatever the curtain brings.

'I've never told anyone why I was against it, but perhaps I will now. It might give you some insight into your enemy'.

She steps into the hut and sits on the chair beside the open door. She has been wrong-footed from the moment she got here. She has never heard Teddy speak so many words in such a short space of time. And more to come, it seems.

'I'm all ears', she says, though she wishes she had said nothing. She can no longer trust her voice not to betray how unsettled she is.

He sits on his chair at his wooden table and takes the toast from the toaster and spreads a thick slab of butter on the two slices.

'I objected to the holiday homes because if they'd gone ahead it would have spelt the end of the line for me as a lockkeeper. All those houses that were to be built would have had their own private marina and their own cruise boat. The pressure for a new, automated lock, opened and closed with the swipe of a piece of plastic, would have resulted in me being out of a job. Maybe not this year or next but there was no doubt in my mind that I'd be an anachronism, sooner or later. That's why I objected. Nothing to do with not wanting holiday homes and everything to do with looking after number one. Which, Sandy, is something you should be doing instead of getting up the nose of every decent person in the parish. A bit less of fixing everyone else's business and a bit more of minding your own for a change would do everyone around these parts some good'.

'Jesus, Teddy'.

'It's true what I say. You've become a nuisance and a pain in the arse to everyone. We were getting on fine before you came along, and we'll get on fine again whenever you decide to leave. Which you will. They all go in the end'.

'Jesus, Teddy'.

It is all she can say for the moment, so she says it a third time.

'Jesus, Teddy'.

'Well I'll be damned, who would have thought Teddy Tiernan would be the one to silence the Keegan woman?'

He pours two mugs of tea, adds milk to both and offers one to Sandy. She takes it and cradles it in her two hands. There are no more words spoken in the hut for some time. Teddy eats his toast and drinks his tea and glances at the back page of the paper and behaves as if she is no longer there. He has been perhaps too blunt and now he is a little lost as to how to proceed, so he sits where he is and breathes in her perfume and glances at the paper and hopes that she will leave soon.

The waters of the river continue to slide over the weir beyond the lock. Out of nowhere a breeze whips in and out of the hut, scattering papers on the floor. Sandy continues to hold the mug in both hands. She hasn't raised it to her lips yet. Her eyes have fallen on a dark stain on the floor that looks like blood, though she guesses it is something less sinister. Teddy's unexpected directness has wounded her deeply. She wishes she could leave but she knows she cannot.

There is something else, an emotion she hasn't anticipated, a sensation that has crept up on her, out of the blue. She knows that there will be nothing she can do to honour this unbidden thought … no, this feeling, for it is not a thought, it is unquestionably a feeling. She knows that as soon as she leaves the hut it will have no room to live inside her. Nor will she afford it any right to exist inside her, for if she does, everything will be ruined. Once, a long time ago, she allowed it in, lost herself within it, gave herself to it. She will not do that again. She will not be so foolish or so weak.

Yet even as she makes up her mind in this regard, she is, for the moment, unable to rise from her chair, incapable of leaving and at the same time her eyes remain fixed on the stain on the floor, for to raise them, to look anywhere but at this precise spot where Teddy puts the soles of his hobnailed boots countless times each day, will be to risk everything, for she has no idea what her eyes might give away were they to meet that man's eyes, and how they might betray her, ruin everything.

'I came here to try to persuade you not to go ahead with the sale', she says.

The words, uttered without conviction, nonetheless give her the strength to rise from her chair. She places her mug on the table and turns to face the open doorway. Her legs feel like they might give way any moment, but she *will* control them, she *will* withdraw with dignity.

'I put a lot of thought into what I was going to say. I knew you were a stubborn man, yet I genuinely believed I could appeal to your better nature, that when you understood, and I mean truly understood, why an industrialised pig farm would be the last thing we want near the village, that you might reconsider. I have no objection to you selling your land. Everyone is entitled to sell their property and make a decent profit from the sale. But our village also has entitlements, and one of those entitlements is to live in a clean environment. For the life of me I cannot begin to comprehend how you could even consider it?'

Speaking her truth has helped her to regain some of her equanimity, but it is a fragile composure that has settled over her and she doesn't feel strong enough to turn to face him.

'Anyway, Teddy, I can see now that I was delusional in thinking I could persuade you. You are worse than stubborn ...' and here she begins to falter, 'you're stupid and ...'

She cannot believe what is happening to her. Her shoulders are shaking and her eyes are filling with tears.

'This is not the real Sandy Keegan you are seeing, Teddy Tiernan'.

She no longer believes what she is saying, indeed it is the opposite of what she has just said that she considers the real truth – that what Teddy Tiernan is in the process of witnessing is in fact the long-buried emotional being that was once capable of loving and of being loved, that was once the very real and very much alive Sandy Keegan.

She could not be more humiliated. Her voice, when she speaks now, is filled with a bitter resentment, yet even as she tries to muster as much conviction as possible, she hears only concession and failure in her words and in her stricken tone.

'You can expect an objection, and you may as well get used to the notion that you're not going to win this one. Goodbye, Teddy'.

Teddy's imposing figure replaces her in the doorframe. He watches her retrace her footsteps along the unfinished path. When it is completed, he thinks, all those who have been giving out about it will see what an improvement it has been. Everyone except Sandy.

He has always had a soft spot for her. He could see through her toughness and her brashness when no one else seemed either able or willing. Even when she was in full flow at the oral hearing last year he sensed a vulnerability behind the brusque delivery. If he wasn't done with women, he would have gone after her then. He would not have given himself more than a fifty-fifty chance of successfully courting her, but she would have been worth the risk. A woman like that is always worth the risk. But his involvement with women is long over and he will not be resuming it, not now, not ever. He likes his life too much the way it is.

He goes back inside to read the newspaper, a little shaken by what has passed between them; an opening of a fissure, an unspoken declaration that will be difficult for both of them to ignore. His odds on capturing the prize have, he suspects, shortened dramatically, and in the most unlikely of circumstances.

What a waste, he thinks, and spits on the floor. The spit lands in the middle of the stain that Tom Curtin's blood made when Teddy knocked him unconscious with one perfectly-timed punch almost twenty years ago. He forgets what the dispute was about – something to do with land, certainly. What he'll never forget is the sound his fist made on impact with Curtin's nose, and how the nose split open like an egg, and Curtin dropped to the floor like a man shot.

It would do him good to punch someone now, just to release the tension that Sandy Keegan has created with her ridiculous pantomime. Instead, he rubs the spit into the stain with the sole of his boot before seating himself at his familiar perch and starting the day proper with a glance at the morning's headlines.

A Surprise Party

The food was being served; large bowls of salad, smaller bowls of hummus and guacamole and plates heaped with ham and cheese and salad sandwiches, carried from the kitchen by Ruth and Patricia out to the larger of the three foldout tables inside the small marquee.

'I have to be getting on', Ross said to Mikey, who was already full with drink. 'I've an early start in the morning'.

His hands had gone dry, a sure sign. He drank the rest of the sparkling water and left the glass down on one of the foldout tables.

'You can't go yet', Mikey said.

The guests who were still inside were summoned to eat. Declan was looking after the drinks, a task he invariably managed to allocate to himself, even at other people's parties. They were a party team, Ruth and Declan, always organising, always at the centre of whatever festivities were going on. Ross could feel the panic rising up inside him.

'I have to go. I promised to drive some friends to the airport for a 9am flight. We'll have to leave at 5'.

'That's mad stuff altogether', said Mikey, reaching over to where Declan was poised with a tray full of drinks. He grabbed two glasses of red wine and handed one to Ross. 'Get this down you and don't be thinking of leaving yet. Sure the party's only beginning'.

Someone Ross didn't know tugged Mikey's sleeve and said something into his ear and the two of them fell into a conversation about the local GAA match the next day. Ross was left standing on his own in the centre of the rough plywood floor, a makeshift effort put down a few hours earlier when it became clear that the weather was going to remain lousy for the entire evening. No one noticed him leave the marquee and walk around by the side of the house, not even Benny McCabe who was taking a leak into the hedge. It was getting dark, which made his furtive exit less problematic than had the party been held a month earlier. Out on the narrow road several dozen cars were squashed in against the hedge on both sides leaving just enough room for a car to pass. He had parked his own car down past the church, thus ensuring an unhindered escape. After years of leaving social gatherings early, he had learned to leave nothing to chance.

The house phone was ringing as he put the key in the front door. He had turned off his mobile hours ago. He guessed it would be Ruth. She'd have heard from Mikey that he'd left and she'd be ringing to give him a telling off. She always had to have the last word, even in the middle of hosting a party. No one else would be calling him at this hour.

'Ross, what's this all about you driving someone to the airport? Since when are you the local taxi service?'

'It's too complicated to go into at this hour, Ruth. I'll explain when I see you. I'm sorry I didn't say goodbye. I went looking for you but I couldn't find you in the melee'.

'Ross, I need you to come back to the party'.

'I told you, I made a promise. Why do you need me to come back to the party?'

'Ross, no one believes that airport lark. We all know what you're like'.

'Fuck off, Ruth. You've some nerve, ringing me and ordering me to come back to your stupid party'.

'Ross, I'm asking you as a big favour to do this for me. The truth is there are a lot of people here who've travelled a long distance to see you tonight'.

'I don't know what that means, and honestly, I don't care. I've to be up at four-thirty. I told Mikey, he's told you. That's the end of the matter as far as I'm concerned'.

'Don't talk to me about Mikey. I'm pissed off with that eejit for letting you sneak off early when he should have known better. Now I'm no longer asking you, little brother, I'm telling you. Get back in your car and get over here. Everyone's expecting you'.

She put the phone down. He went into the unlit living room and sat on the sofa. The familiar outlines of the furniture began to materialise in the gloom as his eyes adjusted to the darkness. Typical of meddling Ruth to be organising something for him that he didn't want. All these parties she threw for other people were really parties for herself, and for Declan to a lesser extent. Mostly, everything she did was a self-centred exercise in ego inflation and ego massage.

The phone rang again. He considered not answering it. He was sorry he hadn't thought of taking it off the hook, but now that it was ringing if he didn't answer it Ruth would assume that he was on his way, and that would merely be putting off the inevitable. He knew from the way she had spoken to him that she wasn't going to let this go. But it wasn't Ruth. It was Fergus.

'Ross, stop behaving like an idiot. No one believes a word of this shite about driving someone to the airport.

Seriously, you really need to get back here. You'll be disappointing an awful lot of people if you don't'.

For the second time in less than five minutes, the phone was put down on him. The evening, which he had anticipated with a sense of dread simply because it involved mingling with people socially, was turning into something more sinister. If Fergus was over in Ruth's, did that mean that Brendan and Orla and Marie were there, too?

The call from Fergus changed everything. Fergus was the family pugilist – an extrovert among a family of extroverts. There was simply no way that he was going to let Ross spoil whatever it was that had been planned behind his back. They were gathered over in Ruth and Declan's and they were united in one purpose, a purpose that appeared to have everything to do with him. He took the phone off the hook.

When he was seven and Fergus twelve, Fergus used to grab him in a headlock when there was no one else in the house and drag him down the stairs to the basement and bundle him into the coalhole beneath the stairs. It was a terrifying place, profoundly dark, draped in thick cobwebs, dense with the heavy, suffocating smell of soot. In there, Ross couldn't see his hand when he held it to his face. Fergus would stay outside the door for a while, taunting Ross, before slowly stamping his way up the stairs, calling as he went, 'Bye Ross, have a nice time down there in the dark. Watch out for the boogie man!' Soon after, Ross would hear the front door bang and an eerie silence would descend on the empty house. Fergus's maliciousness rose to another level when, occasionally, he wouldn't leave the house at all, remaining in the hall when he banged the front door shut. After several minutes had passed he would creep back down the stairs, avoiding the parts that creaked, and he would put his ear to the door of the coalhole and listen. Sometimes Ross would be whimpering like a lonely or injured dog, sometimes he'd be wailing loudly, uncontrollably, but most of the time he'd be too afraid to make any noise at all. Unbeknownst to Ross, as he pressed his entire body against the door, his older brother would have his ear pressed to the far side, less than an inch from Ross's face. He could just about hear Ross breathing. Then, with a sudden and shocking clamour, Fergus would thump the door with his fists as hard as he could and emit a bloodcurdling scream. At this point, the terrified, frozen silence that Ross had been rigidly maintaining would explode into a wail that seemed to emanate from the pit of his stomach. Fearful of what he had unleashed, Fergus would unlock the door and sprint up the stairs and out the front door and would run until he was certain that Ross wasn't following, because even though he was five years older than his little brother and almost twice his size, the fury that sometimes took hold of Ross frightened even him.

Mostly, he left Ross in the coalhole and went up the stairs and left the house. Depending on his mood he could disappear off on his bike and call on one of his friends and not come back till teatime, by which time their mother would have returned from wherever it was she had been, only to discover her youngest son in a pitiful state once again, wailing and sobbing and inconsolable for the rest of the day. Fergus would take his punishment – the withholding of pocket money, the confiscation, albeit temporarily, of his bicycle, a faint-hearted smacking by his inebriated father when he stumbled in from the pub – and depending on the severity of his punishment he would often take it out on Ross at the next opportunity. At the age of sixteen, when Fergus was expelled from school and was packed off to boarding school, the coalhole saga finally ended. Ross was eleven.

'Ross, open up!'

It was Fergus, banging on the door with his fist, just like in the old days of the coalhole. He'd left the engine of his car running and the headlights flared into the living room.

'Open the door, will you? Have you any idea how much you are screwing things up? What in Christ's name is wrong with you?'

Ross turned the key and opened the door wide. He was blinded by the headlights.

'I'm not going back to the party, Fergus'.

'Yes, you fucking are. If I have to drag you kicking and screaming, you're fucking coming'.

'Drag me back, so'.

Fergus stared at his brother. He actually considered grabbing him in a headlock, as in the old days, and dragging him to the car, but the notion evaporated as rapidly as it had entered his head. Fergus was carrying twenty kilos that he didn't need, that he would have been better without. Ross on the other hand looked like he could take him apart with one hand tied behind his back.

Fergus's phone rang. It was Ruth.

'I'm at the door of Ross's house, Ruth, and our selfish prick of a brother is refusing to come back to the party'.

He kept the phone to his ear and turned to look at Ross.

'It may interest you to know that Ruth has spent weeks organising this shindig for you, and at considerable expense. It might also interest you to know that your entire fucking family is over there'.

'Sinéad is over at Ruth's?'

'Yes, you asshole, Sinéad, all the way from Melbourne. What do you think of that, you selfish bastard?'

On the other end of the phone, Ruth had heard everything.

'You're making things worse, Fergus. Try and persuade him to invite you in for a beer. We'll shut up shop here and come on over. If Ross won't come to the party, the party will have to come to him'.

Fergus shoved his phone into his back pocket. 'At least invite me in so we can talk about it'.

'I've no interest in talking to you, Fergus. To be honest, I can't believe you all went and organised a party for me without asking me if I wanted one'.

'We didn't ask because we knew you'd say no. The only way we could do it was behind your back'.

'Well, it was a shit way to do it, and I take no responsibility for any of it. You organised it, you can deal with the fall-out'.

When Fergus's car didn't leave, Ross suspected the worst. Quietly, he let himself out the back door and climbed the low hill behind the house. From there he could see Fergus's car and the driveway down to the slip road and all the way across the valley towards where Ruth and Declan's party was either in full swing or, more likely, was heading his way. He stepped behind a tree and, turning his back to the house, lit a cigarette and drew heavily. His thoughts turned to his baby sister.

Sinéad had been a late and unexpected arrival and was only three when their mother died suddenly. Ross had just turned fifteen. Their father had never featured much in any of their lives and now that his wife was gone, he became more like a drunken lodger than a father. Ross devoted himself to looking after Sinéad. She was a emotionally fragile child and if it hadn't been for the care and the nurturing received from Ross, she may well have ended up in an institution. That's been her view for a long time. Leaving Ireland, leaving Ross, would have been impossible had Ross not distanced himself from her once she had left school and commenced her nursing studies. She knew it was his way of letting go, of allowing her to find her way in the world, of finally going in search of refuge for himself. She understood the need that was in him and while she grieved his slow departure from her life, she never once let on how much the loss affected her.

With Ross gone from her, it was inevitable that she would go away once she had completed her studies. She had no relationship worth talking about with any of her brothers or sisters. She couldn't even bear to be in Ruth's company. She loathed the idea of returning home, for her life in Melbourne had turned out well. That was where her present and her future lay, as far away as she could get from her family. She wasn't to know how deeply Ross had gone into himself, how difficult it had become for him to have any kind of social life. Had she known that a surprise party was the worst possible present she could give to him she would not have agreed to travel. She hadn't known because nobody knew.

He heard the hum of the convoy at the same time as he saw the headlights in the distance, a long line of cars approaching from the far side of the valley. He considered moving further away from the house, deep into the protection of the dark night. There was a ruined farmhouse several fields away he could take shelter inside, for the rain had begun to fall again. He could stay there all night if necessary, seek out Sinéad tomorrow. His head and his heart were at one – both knew what was the right thing to do, yet knowing the right thing to do was not always helpful. Instead of bringing clarity it often invited confusion. He lit another cigarette and pondered this curious fact. He wondered what all the people he had ever known would make of his dilemma. He wondered would they laugh and tell him to get a grip, or would they try to understand, to reassure, to coax him out from behind the tree which had already begun leaking rain onto his head and his shoulders, the skies fully opened now and the promised rain teeming down, spoiling everyone's party.

THE FAR SIDE OF HAPPINESS

I chose my route deliberately, along quiet roads on which there were no pubs. I didn't trust myself not to ruin another day. The morning was cool, the park eerily quiet, but I was at the gate now and maybe it would lift me out of the mood I'd crawled into and couldn't get out of. Strolling around here had to be better than moping about the flat, feeling guilty about the abandoned shop, the disaster it had so rapidly become; and a wiser option to the main drag where the pubs would be calling to me.

I took a right inside the gate and walked the outer loop. It's a small park and I was back where I started five minutes later. I hadn't passed a living soul. Dead ones, no doubt, though none were of a mind to reveal themselves.

I headed inwards, towards the pond. Three old men were sitting and talking on a bench in the lean-to, in from the rain. One of them looked remarkably like my father, though my father would never have been found on a bench chewing the fat with two other old guys. Not his style. Besides, he was long dead. The likeness was nonetheless striking. I wanted to stop and listen, to hear if he sounded like my father, but loitering in their presence would have been intrusive so I left them at it, the two old men and my father who wasn't my father, and crossed the path that divided the park in two and completed the loop on that side, stopping outside the playground to observe a girl of four or five sitting on one end of the wooden seesaw. Just the other week I'd come across a photo of a five-year-old me, sitting on an earlier model of this seesaw, in this exact spot. I had no memory of it, just the photo to prove that I had been here all those years ago.

The girl was watching her older sister climb the steps to the top of the slide. The sister sat down, issued forth a loud *whoop* and launched herself down the slide on her wet bottom. Her mother, who hadn't been paying attention, who had in fact been staring at something or someone in the distance, turned to her elder daughter and told her off. The younger sister began to cry. The mother, seeing me standing there caught up in these small, insignificant events, gave me a look that said, *don't you be staring at my daughters.* I raised my arms as if in supplication, as a gesture of innocence, but she was having none of it. If anything, my odd gesture made her more suspicious.

A squad car stopped at the back gates and two guards got out and walked to where a man I hadn't seen until now was taking shelter beneath a large, ancient sycamore. There was a brief exchange of words, then they led the man to the car, put him in the back seat and drove away. It was as if the Stasi had rolled into town. It didn't help my mood, that's for sure.

I turned and exited the park by the main gate and beat a retreat in the direction of Upper Rathmines Road, a regular haunt of mine when I was in my twenties. As I walked I thought about the shop and whether there had been any customers and why I wasn't there to open the door and let them in. I thought about the misery the venture had created in such a short space of time and the worse misery it was about to fling my way. It seemed to me that I was destined to make foolish decisions until my day was done.

I passed the house where a friend of mine had lived before he died. Poor Brendan. At least I couldn't blame myself for that. Brendan's departure from the world was a decision no one knew anything about until it was too late. His parents never came to terms with it. They still grieve, twenty-five years on. I know this because they send me a mass card every year. I stood in front of the house and I looked up at the top floor window and wished I hadn't, for behind the long, curtain-less window, gazing down at me, stood a motionless figure, female, mid to late thirties, with long dark hair and wearing a pale blue dress. She was looking at me with a fixed, concentrated stare. I didn't know who she was, but her presence there, so unexpected, and her gaze, nakedly aggressive and challenging, spooked me and sent me once more on my way. They say it's a myth that you can feel someone's eyes on your back but I swear that I could feel hers on mine as I continued my journey northwards towards the post office. I urged myself to keep walking and to not look back, but the temptation was too great. When I did, I was relieved to discover she was no longer at Brendan's window. I hoped she wasn't on her way down the stairs, heading my way.

At the junction beyond the post office I turned left, but rather than undertake the epic journey that was the long and linear Rathgar Road, and the uneasy journey that would be, passing as I would the house where I'd lived with Emily, a house I'd avoided passing for several years following our acrimonious break-up, I crossed the street and headed up to Kenilworth Square and made straight for my childhood tree and, without thinking of what I was doing, I began to climb it as if I had been propelled back in time to when I was thirteen or fourteen, when I climbed it every time I visited the square. I had no actual memory of this but I knew I had done so, over and over again. Back then I always made it to the top, from where I could look down on the playing fields, the tennis courts, the cricket pitch, the pavilions. Now I stopped halfway up, for the tree had grown into something of a monster in the intervening years and I was not about to risk my life by slipping and falling down through its branches. I settled on a mature, sturdy branch, hidden from view within the tree's private and safe cocoon, and I reflected on how my entire adult life had been affected by my inability to remember. Mostly I tried not to dwell on this memory loss, for it was the source of an odd type of grief and thinking about it was guaranteed to send me on a downward spiral. Always, without fail, the more I thought about it the sadder I became. It affected my life more than anything else.

I don't know how long I stayed up there. I do know that a boys' rugby match started, and finished, for I heard the constant cries and calls of the boys and the referee's whistle and I heard the thud of the ball being kicked and I heard lots of shouting from the coaches and calls of encouragement from the mums and the dads and the occasional cheer as a try or a penalty was scored.

And then it was over, and the square became quiet again, and sometime after that I made the perilous descent – coming down is always harder than going up – and left the square and cut across to Leinster Road, fleeing the absence of memories, grieving their loss. Having almost no memories made me constantly wary of who I might meet, and in that respect Rathmines, where I was now heading, was a minefield, for much of my past was spread out all around me there.

Fragments. That's all I had when it came down to it. Emily, and those eight years we spent together, yet all I had to latch onto was her inimitable laugh and a string of incomplete, fuzzy images. The rest is indistinct, unreachable. Likewise Brendan. Best friend for a decade, yet he exists as little more than a cardboard cut-out in my mind. In ten years from now, I will have forgotten where I was living when I was running my little shop into the ground. I may even have forgotten all about my little shop.

There's a desk in the library that has my initials carved on it. When the librarian pointed it out to me one day last month, it meant nothing. It was a double embarrassment, because I hadn't remembered the librarian either, despite the fact that we'd gone out together when we were in college. It was her who had found my initials. All those years ago and she remembered me telling her how I'd studied for my Leaving in the library and how I'd left my initials on one of the desks. When she was appointed branch librarian one of the first things she did was look for the desk with GK gouged into the wood.

I stood by the desk now and tried to recall something, anything, about the seventeen-year-old boy who had sat here. What was he like? Did he have hopes and dreams? If he did, he could not have envisaged the disastrous series of wrong turns that lay ahead, waiting to floor him.

Pamela, the librarian, waved to me from behind the counter. She was busy with borrowers and returners. She signalled to her watch, stuck two open hands in the air to indicate ten minutes, then pointed downstairs. When we met a month ago, here in the branch, she spoke about our time in college and I pretended I remembered. She told me she had two sons, both in Trinity, one in his first year, the other doing his finals. She told me that she was waiting for her divorce to come through 'any day now'. It was a lot to take in. I comforted myself in the knowledge that it would not be long before I had forgotten Pamela and her reminiscences all over again. Having no memory did occasionally, and conveniently, have an upside.

Next time, I mouthed, then turned my back and descended the stairs. I passed two elderly women in the lobby, bent towards each other, caught up in an intense discussion. One of them, small and of slight frame, wore a purple coat not unlike a coat my mother used to wear in her later years. How odd it was that I could remember many of my mother's coats. Very little else about that dearest of women, but her coats lingered, just like Emily's laugh. This purple-coated woman also bore a slight resemblance to my long-dead mother, and not just her small stature and her slight frame – something about her expression, her eyes clear and blue and bright and open to the world, reminded me of Mam. The resemblance was nowhere near as striking as the old man in the park was to my father but it was close enough to catch me out, to unsettle me further.

I took a left, in the direction of my old school. Passing the walls and the railings I fought against a powerful urge to look left, to where the large rectangular playing field stretched up and back to the school buildings. Hidden in there, and hidden in my damaged brain, were memories I was sure I didn't want to remember. I wasn't entirely sure why, I had never known why, but I had always known that there was something that should not, at any cost, be remembered. I had been happy in school, I believed, but I had also been something else, something the far side of happy. What that had been I did not know and did not wish to know. For once, I was glad I had no memories.

Across the street was Richmond Hill, the road I grew up on. I knew it was unwise, considering the mood I was in, but I couldn't stop myself. I crossed the street and walked along the footpath towards the house where we had all lived.

According to my brothers, the old house had been altered beyond recognition shortly after we left, with partitions everywhere and a dozen tenants packed in like sardines. The long front lawn that filled up with daisies in the summer was now a narrow run of crude concrete. The ornate wrought-iron gate had been ripped out long ago and replaced by nothing but the space it left.

The front wall. The first tree I ever climbed. All gone. I took my phone out of my pocket and took a few photos, then stood staring up at the house. I was filled with uncertainty. I didn't know where I was heading next and I didn't know what I was going to do when I got there.

I did know one thing – I would never again stand at this spot if I lived to be a hundred. Nothing had been gained by coming here and I would gain nothing by coming back. The past was the past but more than that, it was an entire life beyond my reach. I would no longer torture myself over its loss. *I will live in the moment.* I remember clearly saying that to myself, repeating it over and over, like a mantra, in the hope that the thought would stick, though I guessed it wouldn't. I turned my back on my childhood home then and I walked down Mountpleasant Avenue towards town, towards where my abandoned shop was waiting for someone to take responsibility. All the while I walked I tried hard to live in the moment. It wasn't easy – I knew I was trying too hard – but it was the best I could do and at least I was trying. That is what I was thinking as I walked into my new life.

Gerry Boland is a Dublin-born poet, short story writer, children's author and non-fiction writer. His first book, *A Pocket Guide to Dublin* (Gill & Macmillan) appeared in 1994, followed in 1999 by *A Stroller's Guide to Dublin* (Gill & Macmillan). His debut poetry collection, *Watching Clouds* (Doghouse Books) was published in 2011. In the same year, *Marco Moves In* (O'Brien Press) appeared, the first book in his 'Rather Remarkable Grizzly Bear' trilogy. *Marco Moves In* was nominated for an Irish Book Award. 2012 saw the publication of books two and three in the same series, *Marco Master of Disguise*, and *Marco Moonwalker*. His second collection of poetry, *In the Space Between*, was published by Arlen House in 2016, and his first collection of poems for the young reader, *The Secret Lives of Mothers*, appeared later that same year. He has been living in north Roscommon since 1999 and was Writer-in-Residence for the county in 2013 and 2014. He writes an occasional column on writing for the *Roscommon Herald*. *The Far Side of Happiness* is his first book of short stories.